A LOAD OF OLD BONES

A rather unusual vicar and his most singular cat and dog take a nostalgic romp through a mythical 1950s Surrey, where murky deeds and shady characters abound. Moving from the inner city to the country, the Reverend Francis Oughterard is anticipating an easy life and a bit of peace and quiet. Instead he becomes entangled in a nightmare world of accidental murder, predatory females, officious policemen, wrathful parishioners and a drunken bishop. As the vicar's life spirals out of control it is up to his supercilious cat and bone-obsessed hound to take the initiative and save his skin.

A LOAD OF OLD BONES

A LOAD OF OLD BONES

by

Suzette A. Hill

Magna Large Print Books
Long Preston, North Yorkshire,
BD23 4ND, England.

British Library Cataloguing in Publication Data.

Hill, Suzette A.
    A load of old bones.

    A catalogue record of this book is
    available from the British Library

    ISBN   978-0-7505-2842-9

First published in Great Britain by Bear Books 2005

Copyright © Suzette A. Hill 2005, 2007

Cover illustration by arrangement with
Constable & Robinson Ltd.

Published in Large Print 2008 by arrangement with
Constable & Robinson Ltd.

Magna Large Print is an imprint of Library Magna Books Ltd.

Printed and bound in Great Britain by
T.J. (International) Ltd., Cornwall, PL28 8RW

For my mother, Pamela,
who used to tell me stories.

In grateful memory.

Acknowledgements

I should like to thank the Very Revd Alexander Wedderspoon, Dean Emeritus of Guildford, and the Very Revd Peter Francis, Warden of St Deiniol's Gladstone Library, Hawarden, for being so patient in reading the original manuscript and showing such interest and encouragement. My thanks too to Cherry Bentley-Taylor of the booksellers Ledbury Books & Maps for her warm enthusiasm and promotional support. Julian Smith supplied the crossword clue to fit my prescribed answer: his wit is immeasurably sharper than mine in such matters!

1

The Cat's Memoir

It was Bouncer who found the leg. Well, the whole body really, but it was the leg – stout, white, thick-ankled – that had initially caught his attention and caused him to curtail his sylvan rampage. These rampages were a periodic occurrence embarked upon with a mixture of cringing stealth and cavalier bravado. He once told me that they gave him feelings of exquisite triumph, being proof yet again that a gap could be breached in his master's laborious barricades. Once out and in the wood he would wreak havoc upon the rabbits and lesser denizens, crashing about in that absurd slow-witted way until eventually, worn out with futile exertion (rarely did he catch anything), he would slink home or be collared by his protesting ineffectual owner.

Bluff and blustering, the man was possibly even more obtuse than his canine charge, and they suited each other: Reginald Bowler,

11

local bank manager – raucous, dull, pipe-obsessed; and Bouncer his ridiculous mongrel companion. They had what I have heard humans describe as a sound working relationship, an ill-defined rapport difficult for outsiders to grasp. Most evenings you would see them – *I* saw them – floundering around the block: the man with pipe a-glow, jauntily proprietorial of dog and neighbourhood, snapping out soldierly commands (his feet are flat, he never served); and amidst the sparks and noise, straining manically at the leash, Bouncer – oblivious to all except the next lamp post.

And so they would go, leaking and fuming along the pavements until they drew level with me on my gatepost, when things would change a trifle. At this point I generally managed to contrive a mild fracas: a little cat-calling perhaps, a minor skirmish – some light *divertissement* to help the evening along and hasten the mousing hour...

But I digress, and must return to the matter of the leg. You see, it belonged to my mistress. As indeed did the attached body. So when Bouncer came careering up the street bellowing the news around my watchtower I was hard pressed to retain my customary aplomb. As you might imagine, the news was a bombshell and I experienced acute feelings of shock, albeit tinged with the merest quiver of satisfaction. Nevertheless, shock was dominant; and not caring for Bouncer to see it I continued to stare down indifferently at the histrionics being enacted round the base of my pillar.

That pillar, I may say, was not only convenient but eminently comfortable. Convenient because it afforded me an expansive view of most of The Avenue, ranging from the Blakes' bungalow Khartoum at the far end, to the vet's house on the edge of the park, and finally to that appalling monstrosity at the top of the slope belonging to the Misses Veasey which they had the nerve to call Nirvana. Bowler's place was just out of sight but I liked that as it was amusing trying to gauge the precise moment when dog and master would round the bend on their evening foray.

On the afternoon of the leg I had assumed this ritual would be waived, for judging from the yelps emanating from Foxford Wood Bouncer had escaped his flimsy Colditz and was savouring a joyous idyll among the rabbits, intent – to quote one of those human music maestros – on making 'the buggers hop'. Hop they did, so he told me afterwards.

(But I take that boast with a flea's knee, suspecting that Bouncer's capacity for duffing up rabbits is largely in his imagination.) At any rate, I knew that he would be in disgrace and thus forfeit the nightly exercise, and so with a slight sense of disappointment I had settled down to doze in the noonday sun. The stone was warm, its surface smooth and solid: an admirable piece of masonry on which to pass an idle hour.

The value of comfort to a cat cannot be stressed enough. Without it contentment is a chimera; with it life has a quality which dogs – particularly those as limited as Bouncer – can rarely contemplate. My pillar was one of a pair of grandiose posts guarding the long gravel drive to Elizabeth Fotherington's residence. Like several in the neighbourhood the house had been built just before the First World War and seemed to reflect that air of solidity and confidence which, rightly or wrongly, humans ascribe to that era. The same cannot be said of its owner, my mistress.

Solid legs she may have had, but in all other respects she was entirely at odds with the house she inhabited. Edgy, fulsome and witless, she was a constant source of annoyance to me; and my best means of refuge from those crushing embraces was the sanctuary of the high pillar. Facing south it offered an easeful warmth and was sufficiently elevated to ensure protection from pavement vulgarities. I doubted whether St Simeon's perch was half as good as mine, and in any case probably lacked its attendant tree – whose overhanging branches were not so dense as to blot out the sun yet thick enough to create the necessary camouflage. Cats need camouflage. We are prey to dogs, small boys, and petulant householders.

In particular the tree helped to veil my presence from Bouncer. When he bounded round the corner, with or without his asinine master, he was never *quite* sure whether I was there or not. The creature's sense of smell is fairly acute but I sometimes think his eyesight is defective. This may be congenital (one of the several handicaps of the canine condition) or perhaps the effects of the lunatic fringe which cascades from his brows. But whatever the cause it meant that he did not always observe me lurking there, and thus when not in a socializing mood I could remain withdrawn and be spared his frenzied greetings.

Anyway, the leg. There I was that afternoon quietly enjoying my customary post-prandial snooze when suddenly the air was rent by the dog's excruciating tones. As mentioned, I managed to keep my composure and icily directed him to lower his voice. My cool reaction had a sobering effect and he proceeded to recount his experience. It was a fairly lengthy business as he is not the most succinct narrator and much of it was punctuated by demonstrations of how he had beaten hell out of the rabbits. I told him to get to the point which he eventually did.

Apparently he had been resting briefly having first rolled in a mess of rotting leaves and Lord knows what (the pungency was still upon him), when he noticed a large bush to his right. He was just pondering whether it had lamp-post possibilities when he caught sight of something alien protruding from its undergrowth. His eyesight not being of the best, he went over to take a few exploratory sniffs. He said there were a number of flies buzzing around which it was fun snapping at, and that the thing seemed fairly stiff and had a smell which he couldn't quite place. He tried a few tentative licks and thought the texture vaguely familiar; but it was only when he registered the brown leather casing at the near end and saw it was a human shoe that – to use his own words – 'the bone dropped'.

Now, I know Bouncer is none too bright but even he has flashes of perspicacity, and it passed through his mind that where there was one leg there might be two. So he rummaged around a bit and found the second one tucked up in a twisted position under a green garment. It was a dress clothing a female torso to which both legs were attached. He said he was bouleversied by the discovery (my word actually – I think his was 'buggered'); but shock turned to awe when on closer inspection he realized that the brown shoe, the dress, the chiffon scarf wound tightly round the neck (plus the unaesthetic shape of the legs) all pointed to one person, namely Mrs Elizabeth Fotherington, owner of Marchbank House, bane of the local church and its incumbent, and my ghastly mistress!

Why she should be dead I could not think. She had been only too alive the previous evening, twittering around the place in her usual irritating way: moving the ornaments, straightening the cushions, plaguing the budgerigar, crooning and gurgling down the telephone to the vicar, and humming interminably in that high gnat-like voice. In short, she had been her normal maddening self. Nothing untoward, nothing remotely interesting. So what was she doing now, flat on her back under the hawthorn bush dead as a doornail?

As a species we cats are an independent group and in view of my antipathy you may be wondering why I elected to stay. The answer is simple: food and comfort. I have already discoursed on the importance of the latter, and in the realm of food I confess to being a bit of a gourmet (unlike that philistine Bouncer whose idea of a good meal is a tin of Muncho and a gnaw on one of his disgusting marrow bones).

These epicurean tendencies my owner largely satisfied, providing me with a spacious garden full of the things I most admire: the noble catmint, clouds of trailing asparagus, the intoxicating lemon verbena – lush and wonderful basking plants! And in the house there were soft surfaces, plump cushions, sensuous rugs and eiderdowns where I could luxuriate to my heart's content. Being of a foolish and indulgent nature she permitted me these things. Nothing was forbidden, not even the flexing of my claws on those irresistible shiny cretonnes. My meals were served promptly, the menus delicious and diverse. Cream was copious, fish plentiful. In short I lacked for nothing.

Naturally there was a penalty to pay for all this: her presence. I am by nature a reflective cat. She, however, was ceaseless in her chatter; tediously effusive, and as far as I could make out reflected on nothing but the Reverend Francis Oughterard on whom she lavished gross and painful attention. Whether he was as adept at eluding her clutches as I was, it is hard to say. Probably not – guile is not one of his qualities.

However, back to Bouncer and those critical moments when he first apprised me of the afternoon's events. He was clearly in a state of shock (as was I, though naturally mine was the more concealed) and I felt an unaccustomed sympathy as he shifted from paw to paw peering up worriedly through the curtain of that bedraggled fringe. I think that the excitement of flouting Bowler's fences, the exertions of the rabbit hunt and the repellent encounter with Elizabeth Fotherington's corpse, had all taken their toll and he was obviously eager to return to the ministrations of Bowler and his foul-smelling pipe. Nevertheless, I had to speak sternly to him, pointing out that he couldn't just slope off home as though nothing had happened, and that it was his duty to somehow or other alert his master to what he had found.

These injunctions, you understand, were not prompted by feelings of public concern but rather by the realization that the sooner the neighbours were informed, the sooner my feeding programme could be resumed. The people next door had always spoken very civilly to me and on one occasion I heard them compliment my mistress on the lustre of my fur. Thus there seemed a fair chance that once they heard of their neighbour's demise they would take pity on the poor beleaguered cat. Naturally I couldn't expect the meals to be of the same high quality; but circumstances, as they say, alter cases, and occasionally standards do have to be modified. It is all to do with ports and storms.

So I dismissed Bouncer with a gracious flick of my tail and settled down to devise plans for my future welfare. At that stage questions involving the details of my late mistress's death – the whys, whos and wherefores – did not really occupy me. They were to later, but for the time being it was all a matter of *sauve qui peut* (or purr, as the case may be).

2

The Vicar's Version

When the bishop first sent me here I thought he must be mad. They can get like that, bishops. It's the job; it makes them lose their sense of reality and they go a bit peculiar. I had seen it a number of times and thought that might have happened with Clinker. But as things turned out, either by accident or design he was proved to be right. Contrary to expectation the parish does suit me (and possibly I the parish), and – except for one dreadful phase – my time here has been as undemanding as I could wish.

I don't quite know why I entered the Church. It seemed, as they say, a good idea at the time. I am not the most vigorous of people and when I was demobbed I had been in a bit of a state. The war and my military companions had taken their toll: the bombs, the bellowing, the bull – it was all just too much. Therefore when I got my papers (which they seemed eager to give me at the first opportunity) the relief was enormous. But I had no idea what I was supposed to do. My late mother had provided me with a modest income so I was not exactly pressed for funds; but at some point these would need to be supplemented and I knew I ought to be seeking a *role;* carving out a career, climbing a ladder or something or other to *success*. Others were busy at it: opening garages, selling cars, importing nylons. But I couldn't muster an interest in these, or anything really that required entrepreneurial drive. Enterprise is not my forte.

So deciding what to do – what to *be* – was no small problem. It was further complicated by the fact that army life, though onerous, had at least given me a framework and provided a coarse but convenient canopy. Where in the civilian world should I find comparable cover? School-mastering possibly but I had an aversion to small boys – or larger ones for that matter, having seen quite enough adolescent waggishness in the Mess to last me a lifetime. So somehow it was the Church that I drifted into.

In its size, order and hierarchical complexity, the Anglican Church in those days resembled the army but without the latter's licence to kill. I judged that it was an institution into which I might melt anonymously and yet derive from it a modicum of status requiring little effort to sustain. In this I was greatly mistaken, initially at any rate. I had overlooked the fact that we had now entered upon the era of 'muscular Christianity' and as you may have deduced I am not of a muscular disposition.

However, I completed my theological studies and largely through default found myself ordained. Hopes of avoiding the more extrovert aspects of the profession proved vain, and it soon became clear that if I were to achieve even the most modest distinction I should have to become hearty and 'dynamic'. To this end I endured the horrors of the rugger field, challenged my fellow clergy to arm-wrestling bouts in Working Men's clubs, downed endless pints of wind-inducing beer, and led rousing discussions on such crucial questions as 'Would Jesus Have Joined A Union?' or 'Is God Your Tipple?' To some it might have been a challenge; to me it was exhausting.

Nevertheless, it seemed to pay off as my superiors were evidently satisfied with my progress and I was rewarded by being given charge of a large and unsalubrious parish in Bermondsey. Clearly I had overplayed my part. But it was not such a catastrophe as you might think for by now the role of 'Boxing For God' had got me by the throat and I became the zealous victim of my own fantasy. Thus for a number of years I laboured, proselytized and marched under its delusion. Eventually such fervours took their toll and the contrivance collapsed. I went into a decline, became twitchy, depressed and finally ill. Simply, I suppose, lost my nerve – just as I had in the army.

However, I persuaded myself that this was merely a temporary lapse, an aberrant phase brought on by excess of ardour. The Southwark authorities were sympathetic and allowed me a brief sabbatical. And then, just as I was preparing to re-enter the fray swirling the clerical cudgels, they suddenly transferred me out of Southwark and into the neighbouring diocese. The bishop here was Horace Clinker whom I had known some years previously, and he chose to have me assigned to the small parish of Molehill in Surrey, a quiet community as different from Bermondsey as semolina from salt beef.

I was surprised and affronted... After all, had I not built my modest but hard-earned reputation on bringing the Message to the shop floor: drinking with the best of them, thumping out boogie-woogie in the Mechanics' Institutes and generally being a glowing example of the 'relevant and thrusting' Church Militant? To be now relegated to this prim backwater was insult indeed – which was why I concluded that the bishop was mad.

3

The Dog's Diary

That cat Maurice is such a supercilious bastard. Yes, he thinks I wouldn't know that word, but as a matter of fact I know quite a few long words and *supercilious* is only one of them. I hear them from my master when he does the crossword or telephones his bank customers. I also know *overdraft, outofthequestion, outrageous, insolvent, certainlynot, disgraceful, mydeargoodlady*. Haven't quite got the measure of that last one yet but Bowler uses it pretty freely so I'll probably get the hang of it. Perhaps if I say it to Maurice it'll start to make sense. Anyway, as mentioned, he really can be so rude. For example, only the other day he made some dire crack about my hunting abilities, suggesting that the rabbits' racing handicaps must shoot right up whenever I appear in the undergrowth. That's just typical of his low sarcastic humour – *wit*, he would call it! I replied coldly that I hadn't seen *him* with any trophies recently and that the mouse population was beginning to look pretty plump and prosperous. He didn't like that and went into a sulk. Caught a raw nerve there!

I don't wish him any harm, you understand, but occasionally I can't help wishing that he would forfeit one of those nine lives by falling off that damn gatepost. That would bring him down to earth all right! It won't happen of course. He clings to it like a limpet, preening, purring, and generally lording it over everyone. Still, a dog can dream... Mind you, he's not awful all the time and sometimes makes me laugh by twirling his tail and making funny screeching noises. When he does that I join in with low growls and we make quite a good row together. The neighbours get a bit shirty, and that old Fotherington starts to play up, accusing me of disturbing her poor pet. Poor pet, my arse! He runs rings round her.

Come to think of it, not any more he

won't. Not after what I discovered the other day! Perhaps you've heard about that: my brave escape, my prowess in the woods (prowess – that's another good word I've learnt from Bowler), me sounding the alarm and dragging my master to view the body. In fact I played a jolly important part in it all. Even Maurice said I was a right little hero though whether he meant it I'm not so sure. You never really know with that cat, and sometimes I *am* a bit slow at working things out. Not too slow of course, just averagely so. Well, I can tell you, once I had taken Bowler to the wood all hell was let loose and the hoo-ha has been going on ever since.

Do you know, there's been so much excitement – what with hordes of police, reporters and gawping onlookers – that I've not had the chance to dig up any of my bones for days. To tell the truth, after finding THE LEG, digging for small thrice buried marrow bones seems a bit tame. I mentioned this to Maurice and he looked relieved, muttering something about an ill wind. He's funny about my bones, always has been. Fish is his thing – though I doubt whether he'll be getting much of that now that she's gone. Serve him jolly well right! He's a spoilt rotter.

As a matter of fact, since the discovery he hasn't been looking quite his lofty self; seems a bit edgy and off colour. Delayed shock, I shouldn't wonder. It must be quite a facer losing his mistress like that. Not that he had any affection for Fotherington – far from it – but he likes his comforts all right and she certainly gave him those. He's probably beginning to feel the draught. Still, he's a clever beggar and he's bound to think of something.

Bowler's been a bit odd too. She was one of his best customers (a good and hefty bank balance by all accounts) and I used to notice that whenever she was about, at the bank or one of those puzzling bridge parties humans are always giving, his voice would get even boomier than usual and that funny word *mydeargoodlady* would be flying all over the place. (Must remember to try it out on Slick Paws sometime.) Maurice used to say that he had designs on her, but I don't know what that means so can't comment. What I do know is that ever since the EVENT a steady flow of whisky has been leaving the bottle. Our evening walks are shorter too and he keeps lolling about doing nothing; even his pipe seems to have lost some of its puff. Perhaps he's sickening for something. It's as well that so much is going on in the wood and at Marchbank House otherwise I might be getting just a teeny bit bored. I do like to have a bit of *life* about me...Whoops! Paw went in it there all right!

Can't help thinking about that so-and-so Maurice. He's not on his gatepost so much these days. As for visiting Bowler's garden, he hasn't been here for ages. The master has a passion for birds, and Maurice used to come and sit on his wall as bold as brass and pounce on anything with wings from midges to magpies. He isn't specially interested in the creatures themselves, it's just part of his general bloody-mindedness. He likes to stir things up. It works a treat: Bowler does his berserk act and has a right little rampage while Maurice prances about caterwauling. Or sometimes, cool as a cold nose, he will crouch stock still pretending to be Felix the Garden Gnome; and then just as Bowler gets to him he leaps into the air in a shower of hiss and spit and shoots off into the lavender spraying dust and grass seeds all over the shop.

It's good fun and although there's all that shindig up at Fotherington's house I'm beginning to miss it. Besides, without having Maurice around delivering his usual commentary on events I can't get their full taste. Keeping a bone to yourself is one thing, but this corpse business really needs another jaw to chew it over with. Don't know where that cat goes these days but I'm a good sniffer so I shall put my nose to the ground and jolly well find out.

4

The Vicar's Version

After a few months in the parish I began to think that Clinker, though quite possibly unhinged, was not actually barking. His decision to send me here may well have been one of those rare flashes of episcopal insight for which one must ever be grateful.

As the weeks passed I began to experience a curious and not unpleasant sensation of air being gently released from taut lungs. There are, you know, certain things whose salutary value one can long be persuaded of – cold baths, firm mattresses, bracing walks, the *Manchester Guardian*, porridge, *The Children's Newspaper* – but whose abandonment brings insidious guilty relief. It is a sort of sinking, cushiony feeling of the kind reportedly felt by women when removing their stays.

Thus it was with me and the Church – or at least that part of the Church which expected its clergy to show a robust and jovial militancy. Joviality is not my strong suit (though I have seen enough to make a competent copy); and – as my superiors in the army seemed fond of pointing out – I am neither robust nor militant. Little by little I started to realize that deep down I had loathed the raucous merriment of my fellow clerics, that I hated Real Ale (or any ale come to that, real or bogus), and that the whole holy venture had been a mistake, a terrible self-induced sham.

So what to do? Nothing very much. Keep head beneath parapet: be kind to old ladies, bless the children, stroke the dogs, preach a soothing sermon. With a bit of luck – and conceivably God's will – all should be well, all manner of thing should be well... What an interesting lady Mother Julian must have been! I think I might have enjoyed her company, which is more than I can say of many women.

It is not that I *dislike* the opposite sex but

31

it has a certain knowing, managerial air which I find unsettling. Nor is it that I have proclivities elsewhere but I just don't seem to have the stamina for any close commitment, least of all a domestic one. The constant noise, the insistent proximities; the tensions of opposing interests, the in-laws, infant paraphernalia, the sulks and tantrums, the kitchen dramas, the adolescent furies – it would all be totally beyond me. In fact even now dwelling on such things I feel a fearful weight of weariness descend.

You see, all I had ever really wanted was a quiet life – plenty of peace leavened with moments of charm and gaiety, the stimulus of a few good books, a little choice music, a glass or two of wine ... a modest enough desire you might think. But so far, whatever the circumstances – school, Oxford, army or Church – it had eluded me. Now, in the year of 1957 in the little Surrey parish of Molehill, amazingly it had started to materialize!

Life here in this leafy enclave moved in a calm and unremarkable fashion. My parishioners for the most part were dull, worthy and mercifully self-contained. The young men did not clamour for my presence on the soccer field, the mothers showed a rare restraint in not thrusting their offspring upon me, and even the Vestry Circle conducted its dreary business with admirable self-sufficiency. (In a moment of kindly altruism I once suggested I should man the tea urn for them but the offer was met with little enthusiasm.) Courteous and undemanding, the congregation of St Botolph's seemed to have few spiritual concerns other than the maintenance of the church spire and the custom and ritual of the Anglican dispensation. It suited me down to the ground.

Of course, I wouldn't say that I was ecstatically happy for ecstasy is not in my nature. But in this staid little place I began to feel a contentment, a sense of ease and wellbeing which I had feared would never be my fortune to enjoy. You will perhaps appreciate, therefore, how awful it was to be seized upon by Mrs Elizabeth Fotherington as the target of her persistent and arch attentions.

No preliminary signals had been given, or at least none that I had been aware of, but one Sunday morning as I was hovering in the church porch after the eleven o'clock service, she made her sudden and fateful pounce. I vaguely recalled seeing her when I first arrived in Molehill; she would sometimes be in church but generally melted away after the service, often amidst a coterie of similarly lavendered ladies. And then for a period she seemed to disappear altogether, but I barely registered her absence as her presence had never really impinged. It would in future!

Looking back on things, I suppose she had been laying her plans for weeks, arranging her opportunities, biding her time. Then when the moment was right she seized it with expert and practised ease. It was a simple enough move, but from that moment, and despite all my attempts at ducking and weaving, I was caught irrevocably in the woman's clutches.

Thus on that Sunday morning, after a few pleasantries about my sermon and the weather, she invited me to one of her 'little soirées'. She had been away, she explained, her annual sketching party in the Italian Lakes, otherwise would have invited me earlier. (Surely there had been ample opportunities; probably waiting to see if I passed social muster.) 'After all,' she observed, 'it was not every day that "this darling parish" could welcome a vicar from the "wilds of bracing Bermondsey!" At this she emitted a high tinkling laugh and with fluttering bejewelled fingers adjusted the tilt of her hat.

I asked if she was familiar with Bermondsey, a question which seemed to surprise her and which elicited further girlish laughter. We changed the subject. After a brief exchange on the topics of psalms and tulips (for which latter she had 'an undying passion') she wafted away smiling and cooing and reminding me to join 'our merry throng' at Marchbank House in ten days' time.

Since arriving in Molehill I had of course met a number of my parishioners socially and had received pleasant if uninspiring hospitality. However, despite my rapidly growing contentment I was still on the social edge of things and felt that Mrs Fotherington's invitation might acquaint me further with my flock. As you may have gathered, I am not particularly gregarious and was enjoying the unaccustomed quiet and space. Nevertheless, total isolation can be a disadvantage. And for a vicar, knowledge of one's congregation is generally considered an asset. Thus it was that I contemplated her 'little soirée' with some interest, mercifully unaware of the appalling consequences it would unleash...

In the intervening days I busied myself with the usual chores – dashed off a couple of bland and reassuring sermons, instructed some lumpish girls in the benefits of Confirmation, racked my brains re the Sunday

School Treat, and ordered some new dog collars from Wippell's. I also bought a piano.

There is a music shop in the High Street run by an ill-tempered pair called Berlin and Beasely (inevitably known locally as the Two Bs). It keeps the usual stock of gramophone records and sheet music but also has a vast conglomeration of second-hand musical instruments from banjos, bongo drums and cymbals to those tiresome little triangles one was always landed with in the school band. All are crammed higgledy-piggledy into its front window and grouped around a central tableau comprising a helmet from the Boer War, a slightly moth-eaten Union Jack, and a yellowing placard advertising His Master's Voice. I believe the fox terrier on the placard is called Nipper but what relevance he has to the flag and helmet, nor yet their connection to the instruments ranged about, I do not know. In fact as I neared the shop that day I was considering going in to enquire. If the girl assistant was there I could satisfy my curiosity without the necessary purchase. If, on the other hand, either Berlin or Beasely was lurking then it might be politic to buy some small item. I gave this matter careful thought, gauging which would be the cheaper, a music catalogue or a vinyl-polishing cloth.

Occupied with such imponderables, I did not at first notice the change in the window display. It was only when my foot was on the threshold and the bell already beginning to clang that I suddenly realized that something was different. Except for the items of the tableau the whole window had been denuded of its usual clutter and in its place stood two pianos: a baby grand and an upright. Draped 'tastefully' on the lid of the former was the fly-blown flag, while the Boer War helmet had been carefully positioned in the middle of its stool. Balanced rather precariously on the top of the upright was Nipper and his wind-up gramophone looking, I thought, a trifle uncertain in his new elevation.

I gazed fascinated at this transformation but was also impressed by what certainly appeared to be the good condition of the pianos. The larger one was ebonized, the other of some sort of maple. Both wore reputable but undistinguished names. Screwing my neck in various directions I was able to locate the price labels and decipher their crabbed inky script: the figures were surprisingly reasonable. The ivories of both instruments were pale and polished – and inviting.

Now, I am not very good with my hands, ham-fisted actually, prone to cutting my fingers and dropping things; but strangely I can play the piano. Not brilliantly, you understand, but enough to amuse myself and it seems other people.

I caught the knack at school under the tutelage of some fearsome little man with a glass eye. He taught me duets which was quite fun but also something of an ordeal. In the excitement of the fast bits he would take out his glass eye and place it on top of the piano where it would roll and rattle in the most distracting way. If a piece was really strenuous he would put his teeth there as well. Glass Eye, as naturally he was christened, gave me a feel for the instrument which has remained ever since.

In the army I think it was my saving grace, my one special accomplishment, and which at least ensured me a share of popularity. I can play by ear and improvise so was in demand at parties, and since I enjoy most things from Scarlatti to Novello and Fats Waller I am also good on 'requests'. The talent was useful in the Church during my muscular phase but then it always seemed more of a duty than a pleasure. Now I was free of that charade. Should I indulge myself...?

Banishing the question of cloth or catalogue, I strode purposefully into the shop, and fixing Berlin/Beasely with a glittering eye (strange, the staying power of ancient schoolmasters and mariners) said imperiously: 'I'll have one of your pianos, please!'

Which one did I settle for? As you might guess, limitations of space and funds dictated the upright; but I was pleased with my purchase nevertheless. Had it been a car it would doubtless have been described as a 'good little runner'. There was also a matching stool with removable seat for storing music scores and for which I negotiated a very decent discount. It was duly delivered a few days later and installed in my rather small sitting room and ministered to by Savage, the blind piano tuner from down the road. It looked quite smart and imposing in its new surroundings, and after giving it a brisk polish and shoving a vase of wilting daffodils on top, I sat down and delivered a vigorous rendering of *The Golliwog's Cakewalk*.

Buying that piano was one of the best things I ever did; and as you will hear it has played a significant and companionable role in my life from that day onwards.

5

The Vicar's Version

The day of Elizabeth's soirée dawned and I made the necessary sartorial preparations: dusting down my second best suit (in a decorous shade of clerical grey), polishing my shoes, picking a slimline dog collar from the new consignment; and to add a raffish dash, selected for my top pocket a handkerchief of virulent yellow. I was quite pleased with the result and that evening, unusually relaxed and confident, stepped out smartly for Marchbank House.

As I walked through the gateway my composure was slightly ruffled by the sight of her cat peering down from its usual perch. I was a bit wary of that cat, having passed it a number of times in the street when it would fix me with a stare of querulous curiosity. I found this scrutiny unnerving, and that night too it seemed to be making its customary appraisal. Clearing my throat I quickened my pace up the drive. I had not gone many yards when I heard from behind me an unpleasant noise.

It was a composite sound – gasps, grunts, heavy panting and strangulated gagging. I turned in alarm, and was nearly knocked flying by Reginald Bowler and his dog. They were moving in lurching tandem, the panting coming from the bank manager, the gagging from the dog (at least I think it was in that order). Straining at his collar Bouncer was dragging his owner with glazed intensity, and they overtook me, scattering gravel in all directions. I think Bowler muttered something, even attempted to raise his hat, but he was hauled on relentlessly and they rounded the corner out of sight. I paused briefly, partly to catch my breath and partly to allow them entry to the house before I caught up. By this time I was beginning to feel a trifle nervous and did not want my arrival on Mrs Fotherington's doorstep to be entangled in the imbroglio of Bowler and Bouncer.

The house was large, solid and Edwardian, with a glass-fronted porch and a white door graced by one of those lion-faced brass knockers. It was set amid attractive lawns and flower beds, and from its open windows I could hear the soft tinkling of a piano. It seemed reassuringly calm and welcoming, and despite the little upset of a few minutes earlier I felt a flicker of anticipatory pleasure and rang the bell.

The door was opened by a maid clad in the conventional black and white and I was ushered into a formal salon. This had the potential for being a very lovely room – good proportions, large windows, handsome pelmets, elegant plasterwork – but was in my view ruined by being fussy and over-stuffed: too many ornaments, too many pictures of questionable quality, a superfluity of rugs and drapery, and a plethora of small tables on uncertain spindly legs. In one corner was a grand piano whose notes I had evidently heard in the drive. It was a glossy elegant Steinway and I experienced a pang of envy as I compared it ruefully with my workaday upright. However, it was being played with less than indifferent skill by a pinch-faced woman whom I vaguely recalled as being one of the more rabid members of the Vestry Circle.

The room resonated with a low buzz of unanimated conversation. There were about thirty other guests – a group such as one would expect to find in Molehill rather than Bermondsey: women in pearls with shiny handbags and neatly coiffed hair; a few men in pinstripes and several in navy blazers; the usual clutch of rather dreary indeterminates – forgettable ladies in bobs and spectacles, alone or with undistinguished escorts in ill-cut flannels. The Veasey twins were there looking their usual sepulchral selves, one or two military types, the local doctor, and me – the diffident, falsely beaming vicar. None of us, I judged, was below the age of forty, and most considerably beyond.

I could not see my hostess immediately but in any case was initially more intent on procuring a drink. It wasn't exactly flowing and the choice seemed limited to fruit punch or sherry. Experience has too often taught me that the former is rarely fortified and so I opted for the sherry. It wasn't very nice. Just as I was registering this fact I suddenly saw Mrs Fotherington on the far side of the room in a flowing mauve dress, bedecked with diamonds and talking to Reginald Bowler.

On seeing me she gave a gay wave of her plump arm and endeavoured to move in my direction. She was balked in this by Bowler who was clearly intent on finishing the conversation. From what I could see there was a brief moment of tension as they squared up to each other: the one intent on departure, the other being as obstructive as convention would permit. Eventually she extricated herself and with fulsome greetings weaved her way over to where I was standing.

'Ah, vicar,' she trilled, 'so good of you to forsake your duties to grace this little gathering. How fortunate, how truly blessed we are!' It had never struck me that my presence was much of a benison to anybody but I smiled and nodded and made the appropriate responses to her enquiries about the vicarage. 'I hope it's not too spartan,' she said. 'The late Reverend Digby Purvis was a widower, alas. His dear wife had the misfortune to be eaten by lions years ago in their missionary days. He lived a life of utmost piety – almost one might say of penitential sacrifice. The house has few creature comforts, he preferred the ascetic life. Indeed,' she continued, giving one of those Tinkerbell laughs that I soon came to know and hate, 'I used to think of that little place as a veritable hermitage!' She touched my arm, adding in arch tones, 'I hope *you* won't be such a recluse, Francis!' I assured her that I would do my best not to be, while inwardly thinking that I was beginning to see the attraction.

'His sermons, you know, were most imp-

44

ressive. Not easy to understand of course, but obviously *deeply* profound. In his latter days they radiated a significance utterly baffling!' She sighed. 'Such spirituality! Don't you think that's too wonderful?' I hesitated, not quite knowing how to respond and also recalling the mounds of empty gin bottles I had found heaped up in my predecessor's tool shed. Instead of answering I smiled and enquired casually how he had died.

'Oh, some liver complaint, I believe...' she replied vaguely, adding with lowered voice, 'such a worthy man, *so* high-minded.'

I felt a pang of sympathy for the late Digby Purvis, wondering what kind of hell he had been inhabiting in those lonely months closeted with his gin and his high mind, penning those incoherent sermons. I was glad I had bought my piano and wondered idly whether my next purchase should be a dog.

However, I had no time to reflect on either matter as at that moment there was a tap on my shoulder and a voice boomed in my ear: 'Ah, padre, monopolizing the sherry I see, *and* our good hostess!' It was Reginald Bowler. 'Can't have it all your own way, you know, cutting other fellows out. I know you clerical chappies – always an eye for the pretty ladies, ha! ha!'

So saying he dug his elbow in the ribs of some particularly plain female who had the misfortune to be standing next to him and leered roguishly at Elizabeth Fotherington. She seemed in two minds whether to be flattered by his compliment or irritated by the intrusion. I was similarly ambivalent. His jovial patronage irritated me but I was relieved to be diverted from my hostess's cloying appraisal of the spiritual life of the Reverend Purvis.

Smarming and palming, Bowler delivered himself of further inanities for her benefit and at my expense. 'You have to watch them, you know, these men of the cloth – dark horses they are, my dear good lady, dark horses!' Braying loudly he grabbed a passing sherry and downed it in a single gulp.

'Oh really, Reggie!' she exclaimed. 'You do talk nonsense. Dark horses indeed! You'll embarrass our guest. Besides, I can see the dear vicar is as open as the day is bright!' She simpered up at me and I smiled bleakly.

Somebody asked Bowler how his dog was. Before he could answer Mrs Fotherington cried, 'Ah that sweet little doggie, what a pet he is! He is being such a good boy in the kitchen. Cook has given him some *special* titbits.'

'Nothing sweet about Bouncer,' snorted Bowler. 'A damned villain that dog is, a damned villain!' He stopped suddenly and in mock horror clapped a hand to his mouth and exclaimed, 'Oh dear! Sorry, vicar. Pardon my French! Forgot you were here. Shouldn't like to offend The Cloth, you know!' Bloody fool, I thought.

The joint attentions of my hostess and Bowler were becoming irksome, and feeling things growing too close for comfort I took a step backwards. My heel connected heavily with something solid, and in the next instant a series of anguished howls emanated from the vicinity of my trouser leg: Bouncer. Sated with Cook's titbits he had evidently sneaked into the drawing room in search of new delicacies. What he had got was a hefty blow from my foot. At the same time there was an almighty crash as the dog veered into one of the spindly tables. The silver bowl containing the fruit punch was sent flying, the entire contents splashing over Bowler's backside. There was an appalled silence.

I stared aghast as the animal squirmed and whimpered, displaying all the symptoms of imminent demise. The eyes of the room were riveted upon me and my victim.

Bowler, all bonhomie gone, glared accusingly and snapped, 'Well, that's a fine thing, I must say!' adding icily, 'I take it you didn't see the dog there.' I doubted whether he had either, or indeed anyone else in the room; but exclaimed that of course I hadn't and was terribly sorry etc., etc. Fruit punch trickling down his trouser legs, he continued to glower belligerently; and then stooped down to minister to Bouncer who, silent by now, stared up pathetically not unlike a hirsute Dame aux Camélias. He looked awful.

Elizabeth Fotherington broke into a frenzy of wailing and general hand-wringing, while from elsewhere there were murmurs of sympathy – largely for the dog, some for the punch-soaked Bowler. Few, I imagine, were for me although one of the military was decent enough to mutter that no one but an idiot would bring a dog to a cocktail party. I was grateful for that and was inclined to agree but continued to maintain my air of cringing apology. People started to drift awkwardly to the door, bidding the hapless Elizabeth goodbye and then moving swiftly into the porch. One of the first to leave was the pinch-faced piano player, relieved no doubt to get the chance to give her plodding fingers a rest. Others soon followed, and with a crunching of feet and tyres on gravel they were away. The 'little soirée' was at an end.

A small group of us remained: Bowler of course with the afflicted Bouncer, Elizabeth and one of her house guests, myself, a couple of other people I didn't know and the Veasey twins. One of the latter briskly took charge, directing that the vet be called immediately. 'No,' her sister contradicted, 'the creature will have to be taken there. It's Robinson's late-night surgery. He won't come out.'

Bowler looked impatient and said testily, 'Drat! I shall have to call a taxi. My motor's in dock and I certainly can't carry the poor little brute.' He shot me a look of smouldering reproach. I suddenly brightened, realizing how I might be of use and possibly retrieve a bit of my lost status.

'Don't worry!' I cried eagerly. 'My car is right outside my gate. It won't take a moment to bring it over. We can be at the vet's in ten minutes. Better telephone ahead to say we're coming.' Not waiting for an objection I hurried from the house, trying my best to look firm and purposeful, and strode down the drive glad to be free of that oppressive room. Maurice, as I had heard him called, was still on his gatepost and stared balefully as I passed but this time I

49

was too preoccupied with my mission to be unsettled by a peevish cat.

When I returned with the car they were all assembled in front of the porch; Bowler in the middle looking damp and disgruntled, sodden trousers furled around his thin ankles. He was carrying Bouncer whose earlier whimpering had been replaced by grumbling grunts. I bundled master and dog into the small back seat and said goodbye to my hostess. She had by now recovered her spirits and bade me an effusive farewell, babbling something about a knight in shining armour. In the circumstances I thought the analogy a trifle excessive but, as I was beginning to learn, there was much that was excessive about Elizabeth Fotherington.

I don't think Bowler liked the bit about the knight in armour. Glancing in the driving mirror, I caught him scowling fixedly at the back of my neck. He had taken out his pipe and was making clumsy attempts to light up. This was followed by a gurgling snort. It could have been either dog or master. However, the source was immaterial: as long as neither threw up I didn't care. As it was, I was already worried about the sticky patch likely to imprinted on the upholstery. So with a brisk pump on the accelerator the car shot forward and we arrived at the vet's in double quick time.

The last of the evening's clients were leaving and Robinson ushered us in himself. He glanced quizzically at Bowler's clammy trousers but said nothing. I offered to stay in the waiting room.

'No, no,' he said genially. 'You can come in. Bouncer won't mind, he enjoys an audience. Besides, we can always do with benefit of clergy!'

'Can we?' said Bowler drily.

We trooped into the surgery, where Bouncer was put on the table and duly examined. He was surprisingly biddable, allowing himself to be poked and prodded, and at one point seemed about to nod off.

'He'll live,' announced Robinson cheerfully. 'Nothing much wrong here – always makes a drama! Bit of shock and bruising and he'll be pretty stiff for a few days. Still, I'll have to bandage that back leg – it received the full brunt of the kick and there's quite a graze.'

'I didn't kick him!' I broke in indignantly. 'I simply stepped back and...'

'As good as,' muttered Bowler. The vet affected not to hear and busied himself with

51

bandages. I couldn't help noticing that in the course of drying, the fruit punch on Bowler's seat and thighs was beginning to turn a pale amber. I hoped that Robinson hadn't noticed but could not be sure.

'The problem is,' he said, deftly securing a wad of padding to Bouncer's leg, 'he won't like this and will try to tug it off. But it's got to remain in place for at least two days.'

'Well, you can't expect me to go round like a nanny constantly pinning him up,' protested Bowler. 'I've got important matters to attend to!'

'We can put him in a protective collar,' Robinson explained. 'There's a new device from Scandinavia, not many of them about yet. It looks a bit funny, rather like an inverted lampshade, but it does the trick. Stops them getting at the patch and it's surprising how quickly they adapt.' He went over to a cabinet and pulled out a large box. 'The suppliers normally send white ones but they must have run out or something and they've sent us a consignment from Paris instead. They're just as good but a different colour – pink actually. Something to do with their poodles, I suppose.'

He took from the box what looked like a large poke-bonnet or indeed, as he had described, a lampshade. He laid it on the table and we regarded it in silence. Bouncer sniffed at it curiously.

I had not seen one of these before and started to smile. Bowler must have seen me smiling for with scarlet face he suddenly rounded on the vet and in a voice of thunderous fury bellowed: 'Look here, Robinson, if you imagine I am going to allow a dog of mine to mince about wearing a pink hat like some frigging fairy, you've got another think coming!'

There was a long silence. And then from the table Bouncer stared up at the three of us. He belched loudly.

6

The Cat's Memoir

It never ceases to amaze me, the sheer duplicity of human nature. How fickle and manipulative that species can be! Those neighbours of Fotherington for example, who had seemed so appreciative of my charms ... far from being receptive to my overtures they treated my plight with a boorish indifference bordering on rank hostility.

Such ill nature was not apparent when my mistress was alive and I can only conclude that their former blandishments were simply a means of ingratiating themselves with that addled woman and getting their grasping hands on what Bouncer would call 'a slice of the dosh'. She used to shower them with lavish presents and provide their obnoxious offspring with treats and buns. I suppose they thought they were on to a good thing. Talk about cupboard love: if that didn't take the blue sardine! They showed themselves up as completely two-faced and I was required to rethink my entire strategy. It was really too bad.

However, being a resourceful cat I quickly concocted a Plan B in pursuit of which I started to make a reconnaissance of the vicarage. As a place of permanent refuge this had a certain potential – although compared to my late mistress's abode it was of course a modest property; and peering through the windows I observed a ramshackle disorder not normally to my taste. Beggars, however, cannot be choosers and I did spy a few promising nooks congenial to a cat of my independence. It might suit moderately well. Already I felt detached from my current menage. Cats have few nostalgic ties. We are designed for freedom and self-preservation and cannot be encumbered by the con-straints of undue sentiment.

By my standards the vicarage garden was small and spartan: little evidence of that luxuriant catmint gracing Elizabeth Fother-ington's winding paths. However, there were fields at the back and it abutted on to a size-able graveyard. I had never really noticed this before, having had little occasion to wander beyond the area of The Avenue, but it could, I thought, yield all manner of plea-surable possibilities.

There were for example tombs galore: their surfaces ideal for summer slumbering, and their shadowy angles perfectly set for the concealed ambush, the brisk pounce on passing mouse or marauding dog. Every-where there was camouflage (whose value, you may remember, I have already remar-ked): long grass, thick dark yew trees, deceptive laurels, trellises of ivy and swathes of trailing bindweed. In the neater parts where the grass was clipped there were mounds of freshly dug earth sometimes decked with flowers, its texture fine and crumbly and ideal for good scratchings or attending to matters of ablution. In fact the more I examined the place the more enticing it became.

Its quiet isolation had further appeal although I did rather wonder whether I should miss the little dramas of The Avenue – particularly those bracing skirmishes with Bouncer and his idiot master. But I assumed the graveyard would provide its own brand of drama: diggings, processions, the panoply of cope and fluttering surplice – spectacle enough to feed a feline curiosity. Besides, were I to weary of such novelties I could always return to Bowler's garden and madden him by playing the Wall Game.

But it was all very well dreaming of grave-yard delights. What about the vicar, Francis Oughterard? Would he prove a suitable host? It was essential I had someone congenial this time, not a babbling ninny like my late mistress. From what I had observed he seemed an inoffensive creature but one could never be sure. Being a conservative cat I dislike constant change and did not relish further upheaval should he prove otherwise. I would quiz Bouncer on that score as I knew his master had some link with the church. Certainly he was always trekking off there on a

Sunday (Bouncer being left behind gnawing one of those repellent bones), so the dog might have learned something of its incumbent. His habit of referring familiarly and unsubtly to Oughterard as 'Old F.O.' at least implied a presumption of knowledge.

In all events, I knew I had to proceed with the greatest circumspection. It would have been dreadful to make another error of judgement as I had done with those wheedling counterfeits next door!

Thinking of them returns me to the question of my feeding programme and other domestic matters. For the time being I still had the run of Marchbank House and was thus hardly a refugee (although judging from the gross decline in culinary standards since her death you might have thought so). The lumpen daughter had come to stay – ostensibly to settle her mother's affairs but principally I suspect to ensure that *her* portion didn't go adrift. According to Bouncer, Bowler was the executor. With someone as crass as that in charge I should think all manner of things could have gone wrong.

Being less garrulous, the daughter was not quite so bad as the mother; but she was very large and took up too much room for my liking. She regularly stuffed herself into my favourite armchair and didn't seem to grasp that my sleeping arrangements required the eiderdown and *both* pillows in the best spare bedroom. She had appropriated all of these, which in the circumstances struck me as remarkably inconsiderate. Very often, just when I needed a little repose in the conservatory, I would find her there: sprawled over wills and testaments and eating sandwiches noisily. It was all exceedingly tiresome and I looked forward to the vicarage business being settled.

Returning from exploring the graveyard one morning I encountered Bouncer mooching about in the bushes. He rushed up to me, barking and whooping and throwing himself about as if I had just returned from the North Pole. He was full of questions about my plans; but wishing a little longer to reflect I was disinclined to divulge them immediately. All in good time, I thought to myself. In fact that is precisely what I said to him, adding that he must learn to be patient. He looked at me reproachfully and then tail in air stalked off grumpily muttering something about cats and baskets.

I felt a pang of remorse thinking that perhaps I *had* been just a trifle curt. The foolish fellow meant well. And besides, I did need to ask him about the vicar. So I followed him into the shrubbery where he was busy practising his bone-burying technique, and after a few moments began to purr rhythmically. This has a soothing effect, and when I saw he was sufficiently mollified I told him that I was thinking of taking up residence at the vicarage. He stopped his scrabblings and sat back on his haunches looking thoughtful. And then said casually: 'Of course you do realize he's off his chump.'

'Nonsense!' I snapped, momentarily taken aback. 'He's as sane as I am.' For some reason he seemed to find that statement very funny and rolled about drumming his tail in the dust. When he had recovered I enquired whether he could produce evidence for his allegation. He replied lamely that he couldn't, that it was just a funny feeling he had. I told him that I was hardly impressed by his funny feelings and that he was spreading unnecessary alarm. He protested that dogs possess a sixth sense in such matters. I whisked my tail impatiently and asked him what Bowler thought of the vicar.

'Not much,' he answered. 'He thinks he's a bit prissy.'

'Well, better to be prissy than oafish,' I

responded pointedly. He went back to his digging and I sat pondering the matter.

There is a gossipy little Pomeranian called Flirty-Gerty who used to live near Bouncer and for whom he had a bit of a yen. Short of leg, she keeps her nose close to the ground and is thus a fund of all manner of scandalous titbits. I thought that unlike Bouncer she might know something tangible about Oughterard which could be useful to my assessment. I would get the dog to sound her out on the subject. However, when I put this to him he seemed disinclined and looked shifty. Apparently he had gone off Flirty-Gerty, having been sidelined in her affections by another.

'Who?' I asked with interest.

'William,' he answered morosely.

'Ah, well...' I said. 'I see the problem.'

William was the local patrician: a Great Dane of immense dignity and proportion. If he had Flirty-Gerty under his protective paw then indeed Bouncer stood little chance.

My own feelings about William were mixed. He left me well alone which I appreciated. But there is a difference between being left alone and being entirely overlooked. During my time in this neighbourhood I think I can safely say that I have made my mark. Most creatures, animal or human, are aware of my presence and accord me the appropriate respect (except for those pernicious people next door to Marchbank House). I do possess a certain distinction and this is normally acknowledged.

William, however, seemed totally oblivious of my existence. He would lollop around in benign lordly fashion, great head held high, gazing into the distance with his thoughts apparently fixed on some rarefied matter quite unrelated to his surroundings – let alone to me on my gatepost. He did once lift a languid leg against the base of the pillar but even when I fixed him with one of my sharper glares he remained supremely in-different, almost as if I wasn't there at all. This was distinctly galling – though I have to admit that had he deigned to register my presence in a *hostile* way then it would cer-tainly have been a case of curtains or cat-meat. So I suppose one must take the long view.

Anyway, for the time being Bouncer did not have the ear of the Pomeranian so I decided to quiz her myself about the vicar's creden-tials. Reclining on my sentinel a couple of days later, I heard the brisk clickety-clack of dainty toenails, and guessing it to be the little lap-dog adjusted my features into a suitably ingratiating leer. As she drew close, all prancy and fluffy, I emitted a long dulcet mew calculated to beguile even the most timid of creatures, and awaited her response.

Flirty-Gerty froze. She cast a look of abject terror in my direction and then with an ear-piercing scream shot off down the road as fast as her teetering little paws would carry her. The banshee shrieks rent the air for several excruciating minutes. The sound was amplified by the owner who suddenly appeared around the corner shaking a redundant lead and hurling imprecations. She seemed to imagine that I was somehow responsible. I shut my eyes and tried to think calmly of haddock...

There is simply no pleasing these canines, they are such a contrary tribe – and in view of Gerty's current alliance I thought it politic to withdraw into the safety of the house. This after all might be the one occasion when William came looking for me.

After that fracas clearly a low profile was called for; and for a couple of days I stayed well within the Fotherington domain, emerging only after dark to do a little mouse plundering. Such confinement was irksome for it interrupted my reconnaissance of the vicarage and also meant I was forced into closer proximity with the daughter.

Whereas the mother had been fidgety, mincing and foolish, the daughter had a bovine disposition. Her clumsy movements (twice treading on my tail) and constant requisitioning of the most comfortable chairs were really beginning to get on my nerves. Like her mother she had a propensity to hum: not with the former's high reedy note but in a series of low toneless grunts. At least they heralded her presence, as did the dinner gong in the hall when it vibrated to her heavy tread. Increasingly I found the interloper tiresome and un-aesthetic, and the need to remove myself elsewhere was becoming urgent.

After those two days of enforced isolation I was glad to resume my position on the gatepost. Fortunately there seemed no evidence of William; nor unsurprisingly of Flirty-Gerty. What with one thing and another I had been having a trying time and thought that before proceeding further with the vicar and his property I should give myself a little treat. I would visit the Veaseys' garden and survey its fishpond. I do this from time to time and it is always a pleasurable outing. In the current circumstances such a tonic would be most welcome and I set out briskly.

Despite the grotesque architecture of their house Nirvana, the two Veasey sisters possess an attractive garden and a fine lily-pond stocked with gleaming goldfish. I settled myself comfortably on the pool's edge, and shaded by the overhanging tree proceeded to admire the inhabitants' fishy grace. Languidly I pondered which I should select for my special attention, and as I gazed a particularly choice specimen glided past right under my whiskers. Just as my paw was in an exquisite hair's breadth of its shimmering tail there was a piercing commotion from the direction of the house.

I looked up startled. Grey and angular, the Misses Veasey were advancing upon me like a pair of enraged ghosts; one brandishing a walking stick, the other armed with a vicious-looking rake.

Dividing at the sundial they made a pincer movement around the pond, bearing down on me with remorseless and shocking speed. Feet thundering, beaky noses a-quiver, they launched the assault with military precision. Outflanked and almost outwitted, I made a desperate leap for the tree whose branches were just within reach of my flailing paws. There I dangled absurdly like a cat on a gibbet, swinging, spitting and yowling while those harpies screeched and lunged beneath me. I can tell you, those were tense moments and not ones I care to dwell upon.

The ignominy was compounded by the fact that out of the corner of my eye I glimpsed Bouncer's woolly face peering in from the open gate. Even in my plight I could see that his head was tilted on one side in that inane way of his as he watched, *relished*, my situation. The Veasey bellows were now punctuated by his coarse guffaws which reverberated around the garden producing a trio of nightmare dissonance.

Happily his mirth was cut short: for with a collective bray and a brisk right-wheel, the Veasey twins launched themselves in his direction, the rake-bearer hurling her missile with practised accuracy. It caught him a glancing blow on the shoulder and with an anguished yelp he veered off down the road in a flurry of dust. In his haste he had dropped his mangy rubber ring, which afforded me some satisfaction at least. Alas, it was short-lived, for later that evening under cover of darkness he was able to sneak back to retrieve it; and despite his sore shoulder bore it home in martyred triumph to his lair.

The whole episode left an unpleasant taste in my mouth which returns to me even as I recount it. It was nasty, brutish, not particularly short, and grossly undignified. Events like that are not good for cats.

7

The Vicar's Version

The morning after the soirée dawned bright and sparkling; conditions which doubtless would beckon the untroubled from their beds. I remained in mine. The events of the previous evening capered before my eyes in all their humiliating detail.

As earlier mentioned, until that occasion things had been going very well in the new parish. People were agreeable but incurious and my duties comparatively light; mercifully any internecine friction seemed confined to the mutual point-scoring of Mavis Briggs and Edith Hopgarden; Bishop Clinker had telephoned only once and even my hum-drum domestic surroundings were somehow reassuring in their very ordinariness. In short, Molehill was fast conferring a deep and merciful repose. However, there had been nothing remotely reposeful about that evening at Marchbank House! I stared morosely at the ceiling, wondering whether like the Macbeths Elizabeth and Bowler had murdered sleep.

Still not stirring, I pondered this fear for a time but after a while began to feel less gloomy. How absurd, I thought, to be agitated by an event patently not my fault. If Bowler was fool enough to bring his wretched hound to the party then that was his problem not mine, and he must take the consequences. Admittedly, being the butt first of his smarmy patronage and then of his boorish temper had indeed been galling. But in this respect it was at least satisfying to recall the spectacle of those punch-stained trousers. Serve him right, I thought. Clearly an enemy had been made there but the combination of a wide berth and a cheerful courtesy would doubtless smooth things over. Similarly with Elizabeth Fotherington. Her inane blandishments had irritated me at the time and even permeated my dreams;

but it was silly to allow a foolish woman's style of speech to affect one's mood. The incident had certainly been unfortunate but was really no more than a minor social embarrassment easily forgotten. After all, I argued, it wasn't as if the dog had been permanently maimed or I had disgraced myself in some drunken horseplay. A sense of proportion was needed. All surely would be well. All manner of thing would be well... Comforted by those thoughts I got out of bed, put on a dressing gown and went downstairs to make a reviving pot of tea.

The morning post lay on the mat, and picking it up I noticed an unstamped envelope delivered by hand. It had not been there the previous night when I had got back from the vet's so presumably the sender was an early riser. I opened it idly, assuming it to be from some parishioner requesting a visit or my signature on a form.

It was from Bowler: a curt note enclosing Robinson's bill plus a demand that I pay his dry-cleaning expenses.

As I sat at the kitchen table gloomily sipping my tea and wondering with some intensity where exactly I should like to stuff Bowler's letter, there was a fluttering tap on the window. I looked up and was confronted

by the beaming face of Elizabeth Fotherington.

The upset of the soirée was as nothing compared with the nightmare of the ensuing
weeks. From the moment Elizabeth appeared
at the kitchen window armed with asparagus
and solicitations my life ceased to be my own.
My cherished space was under daily siege;
the telephone became an instrument of
dread. Sunday sermons were an agony:
where should I direct my eyes – to the front,
back, side or centre? On whatever place my
desperate gaze alighted there was *her* face –
staring, simpering, nodding, mapping my
every movement like some crazed carto-
grapher. I am not a particularly confident
preacher at the best of times and Elizabeth's
watchful presence increased the tensions a
hundredfold.

The visits were the worst: they were so
unpredictable. Like those poor unfortunates
in Germany and Poland, you never quite
knew when the knock would come. Pre-
emptive action was invariably foiled, retreat
cut off, bluff called. The gifts, the flowers,
the vegetable marrows, the passed-on
library books, back copies of *Country Life* –
all piled up relentlessly in the hall and in my

dreams. They were the deadly weapons of her battery, for while none was solicited all needed acknowledgement and thus contact.

It was when the knitting started that I thought I should go truly mad. Little things to begin with: tea cosies, dish-cloths, pan holders. These, however, soon progressed to scarves – items of interminable length and garish hue. Fortunately she never got as far as socks but I think they must have been on the agenda.

It wasn't just the attentions per se that made life intolerable, but their public effects. For example, Bowler's original antipathy to me was now fuelled by a quite blatant jealousy. (Why Elizabeth should have spawned such feelings in him goodness knows – a more impossible woman it would be hard to imagine!) It did not help of course that I had declined to pay Robinson's bill; but it was her attachment to me that seemed the root of the matter and really got him going. At first after the Bouncer incident he had remained studiedly aloof, just fixing me with cold stares, but gradually as Elizabeth's attentions became more marked he grew bellicose, actively seeking out opportunities for challenge and dispute. As he was one of the churchwardens these attacks would often occur in committee meetings, prolonging the business and giving embarrassment to all.

Sunday mornings in particular were times of tension. In addition to my torture in the pulpit trying to avoid her avid eye, there would be the awful business of the church porch...

The service over, it was the convention that I took up my position at the main door murmuring pleasantries and shaking hands with my departing flock. I used to rather enjoy the ritual. As with actors, and possibly teachers, those post-coital moments were times to be savoured. Feelings of relief would mingle with – if one were lucky – satisfaction at a job well done, and an almost euphoric sense of release would descend. (At the start of things the congregation seemed the potential enemy: truculently poised to snore, sniff or walk out. By the end they were dear friends whose departure one almost regretted. In the porch one might promise them anything: in the pulpit one prayed they would never ask.) This pleasant little epilogue would be enhanced by the prospect of a modest luncheon and a stiff restorative. Thus the ceremony of the porch was both a fitting coda to the morning's prayers and a prelude to a restful afternoon. Bowler and Elizabeth spoiled all that.

The instant the service was over they were up and running. Well, sidling and elbowing really. Elizabeth, eager to be at the centre of things, would be intent on establishing prime position whence she could also pluck me by the sleeve and issue wheedling invitations for 'some refreshing Sunday sherry'. Bowler, equally set on stopping her, would place himself in such a manner as to inadvertently block her way. If successful he would then steer her with grim briskness towards his car. Looking back on things I now realize that these Sunday contests held good betting material – but at the time I was too agitated to enjoy the sporting angle.

The mêlée that these skirmishes caused at the narrow junction of aisle and porch was extremely irritating and made worse by the fact that the congregation – normally phlegmatic and unobservant – was beginning to notice. Quizzical, even amused looks would be cast, and my normally bland smile would harden into a rictus of embarrassment. Generally by dint of sheer cussedness Bowler would outmanoeuvre Elizabeth. But on one occasion he had been slow off his mark and in a moment of weakness I succumbed to her offer of sherry. Pursued by a gaggle of twittering cronies she tore off eagerly to prepare the decanters, and puce in the face Bowler gave me a look so malevolent that I nervously wondered whether I should transfer my account to the Guildford branch.

I was also terrified that my name might become coupled with hers. So frequently had she been seen with me in public that there could well grow an assumption that we had more than a little in common. Insidiously a feeling of doom began to creep upon me as I realized that my whole edifice of contentment was in mortal peril. Elizabeth Fotherington's clinging awfulness, Bowler's insane jealousy and his relish for making mischief, the pitying mirth of some of the congregation – it was all too much and too dreadful. Where would it end? I could not bear to think that my yearned-for peace was about to be so cruelly shattered.

The piano brought occasional solace but the moment I ceased playing the anxieties would come thrusting back. I racked my brain for some solution but nothing offered itself. Could I perhaps go to Clinker and request a transfer?... But what would that achieve? Probably a posting as dire as the last, and in any case could I really face further uprooting and all the tensions of resettlement? The prospect filled me with a terrible fatigue. Damn it, I fumed, I *like* it here! Why should I be driven out by that woman and her ludicrous nonsense?

Perhaps a heart-to-heart talk would do the trick. In my training days it had always been impressed upon us that 'delicate' situations need firm handling. I seemed to recall that 'clearing the decks' had been the favoured phrase. Truth, we were told, must out: candour was the key to all. I have never been entirely convinced of that dictum, feeling that total truth probably brings as much pain as it is claimed to bring comfort. In any case, the prospect of being closeted with Elizabeth Fotherington while we held a 'full and frank' discussion about our conflicting personal interests was not something that entirely appealed. Furthermore, even if it were the moral course, would it be the *sensible* one? At the back of my mind there echoed some line about hell knowing no fury like a woman scorned. Supposing my kindly meant honesty were to rebound and that far from defusing the problem it simply turned it into something different and possibly worse?

These were questions my brain could no longer cope with. As on certain other occasions I began to experience a slackening of control, a sense of things falling apart and a frightening diminution of self. A wave of helplessness and hopelessness engulfed me. There was of course the ultimate step: leave the Church. Start anew. But start how? Where? With what? A pall of despair descended. I stumbled upstairs, removed my collar and shoes, and fully clothed climbed into bed and closed my eyes.

8

The Vicar's Version

When I awoke dawn was breaking and I realized that I must have slept solidly for a full nine or ten hours. The long rest didn't seem to have done me much good. Mentally I was still jaded, and physically felt stiff and uncomfortable. I got out of bed, threw off the clothes I had slept in, bathed and shaved and went down to the kitchen. Recently I had got into the habit of keeping the curtains closed while I drank my morning tea just in case I should be surprised by another apparition at the window. It was barely seven o'clock so such a visitation was unlikely but I had become increasingly jittery and couldn't take the risk.

I lit a cigarette and thought about my predecessor, the Reverend Purvis. Was it simply loneliness that had made him drink all that gin – or was there a more sinister explanation? Was Elizabeth Fotherington given to hounding harmless clergymen? Had this whole ghastly pursuit taken place before? Did Purvis too fall victim to her predatory sweetness? Topping up my tea I grimly considered his fate. And then, feeling even more depressed, I wandered into the sitting room and sat at the piano. I strummed a little Chopin and then tried to practise my Fats Waller technique but neither would lighten the gathering gloom.

As it happened, I had a couple of weeks' leave owing to me, and my temporary replacement, Basil Rummage, was due that evening. My sister was in the throes of moving into her new house on the outskirts of Brighton and we had arranged that I should go down and give her a hand. However, she didn't want me there immediately and I had decided to spend a few days in Brighton itself, savouring the sea air and gathering my strength for the tasks ahead. Primrose is an exacting organizer and I knew I should be kept busy for much of my stay.

My original intention had been to leave immediately after Evensong the previous day, but the fit of despondency had put paid to that. Instead I would set off that afternoon after some leisurely packing and a bit of tidying up for Rummage. I tried to convince myself that a break at the seaside would do me good but in my present mood couldn't summon up much enthusiasm. Still, if nothing else it would at least provide a temporary respite from Elizabeth's smothering attentions.

I unlocked the back door and went to the garage to top up the radiator. It must have rained in the night as the grass was damp and there was a fresh earthy smell in the air. Wraiths of mist hung about the trees but the sun was already breaking through and the day looked promising. Good holiday weather for those so inclined. At least the drive down to Brighton would be pleasant. I had a slight headache, the result probably of too much sleep the night before, and rather than go upstairs and hunt vainly for aspirin I thought that a short walk might clear the cobwebs and induce a better mood for my trip.

I put on stouter shoes and a light jacket and set off over the fields to Foxford Wood. These fields lie just behind the vicarage and form an attractive rural oasis amid Molehill's gentrified suburbia. I am not much of an outdoor type and rarely walk unless having some specific purpose. But sauntering over the long grass that June morning, smelling the tang of hedgerows, hearing the birds and watching the cows as they placidly ruminated, gave me an enormous pleasure which even now, and despite everything, I sometimes recall.

The sky was clear and the sun was growing stronger, and as I entered the beech wood the light was already dancing in dappled splodges on bush and bramble. Moving through those trees I began to feel the tensions of the last weeks gradually seep away, and caught a little of that serenity which I had feared had gone for ever.

I had taken the main well-trodden path; but on either side of it the wood stretched dense and mysterious, the silence broken only by the occasional flurry of wood-pigeon or the rasping call of cock pheasant. It *smelled* good – damp, woody, mossy. Instinctively I felt in my pocket for my lighter but resisted the urge, the woodland scent being too nice to mingle with tobacco smoke. Instead I sucked a couple of mints which I always carry and watched the rabbits as they idled among the ferns and faded bluebells. Perhaps it was imagination, but I thought I detected somewhere the harsh bark of a roebuck. If I trod carefully I might just get a sighting. I thought it unikely but, vaguely hopeful, strolled on savouring the deep peace of that enclosed and private world.

Suddenly there was a crashing in the undergrowth, a loud snapping of twigs and tearing of roots and branches. The rabbits scattered, pheasants squawked – and equally flustered I turned quickly. It was no roebuck...

It was Elizabeth. She stood there framed between a beech tree and a holly bush, looking like some aberrant version of the Green Man. Flushed and panting, hat adrift, stockings muddied and a bramble clinging to the front of her green dress, she flashed me one of those awesome smiles. I recoiled aghast. Christ almighty! How long, O Lord, how long!

'Oh Francis,' she oozed, 'what an amazing coincidence! I didn't know *you* were an early walker. This must be your little secret. And now I've found you out!'

She beamed rapturously, and still breath-less took a few tottering steps towards the path I was on. I noticed that her plump ankles were thrust into brown cuban-heeled shoes with rather pointed toes. I wondered vaguely about their practicality but was more taken by the fact that her feet looked exactly like a pair of pigs' trotters. I think a kind of hysteria came upon me because I started to giggle. This I could stifle, but not the accompanying smile which she imme-diately took for some sign of reciprocal pleasure. Picking her way carefully, she moved closer, seized my arm and in the usual gushing tones began to talk about the romance of the forest and the wonders of Mother Nature. The noise was ear-splitting.

We walked along arm in arm: she squaw-king and gabbling, me in a trance-like daze. I recall making some polite monosyllabic responses but the whole thing had a surreal-istic quality which makes it difficult to describe. As she talked I was trying in a muddled way to work out what she was *doing* there at that time of day and in such a dishevelled state. Why hadn't she kept to the main path? Why, like some benign wild boar, had she suddenly broken cover from the undergrowth at the side of the track? I couldn't fathom it out and in any case was far too distracted by the barrage of sound at my elbow.

After about fifty yards I suddenly knew that it could not continue. It had to be stopped. Then and there and at any cost. I did not, as they say, see red. I felt no fury, no sense of despair or vengeance: just a cold impersonal necessity.

It happened quite quickly. Looking down I saw the long blue chiffon scarf draped across her shoulders. It went well with the green of her dress. Lightly I laid my hand on the back of her neck. She looked up in surprise, and possibly with a gleam of pleasure – though I can't be sure as everything was so swift. I took the scarf, and in one deft movement (unusual for me) wound it around her neck and pulled. Tighter, tighter... And then much tighter.

I remember looking up at the tall trees, lovely in their arching outlines, and the foliage all lacy. There was a gap in the leaves and I could see a clear vibrant patch of sky. It was so blue and so beautiful. A group of pigeons scudded across, swooping and twirling; and above them I could just make out a glinting movement and an arc of frothy skein. To be up there, I felt, riding the sky, spiralling up into the clouds and beyond must be very heaven! Wings shimmered, birds and slipstream merged. The blue shone, the leaves danced...

And then there was this heavy dragging weight in my arms. And lowering my eyes I saw Elizabeth like a collapsed doll, slumped and lolling. The rakish hat, still secured by its hat-pin, tilted drunkenly over her face; and her legs, with their little trotters, splayed out stiffly amongst the spent bluebells. There was not a breath of movement.

You know, when you have some exacting or dangerous task to perform such as dismantling a mine, untangling barbed wire, cleaning a rifle, staunching a wound or dispatching a dying animal – anything in fact requiring crucial care – emotional feelings such as fear, pity, disgust, are entirely absent. You concentrate exclusively on the mechanics of the job: tying the right knots, finding the vital spot, selecting the correct screw or scalpel, twisting the wire properly. The only thing that matters is getting it *right*. Thus it was with Elizabeth: my pre-eminent concern was to deal efficiently with what had been done. Other instincts played no part.

I lugged the body some yards off the path and laid it under a conveniently large and shrubby hawthorn bush; replaced the hat over her face, folded her arms and straightened her dress. The ground was covered in swathes of bracken and I wrenched these up and arranged them carefully over the body, embellishing the hawthorn's camouflage. Then, just as I was about to leave, I suddenly noticed what looked like her handbag. In fact it was a pair of binoculars with a long strap but minus their case. I was a bit nonplussed by this, not sure whether to leave them there shoved under the bush or take them with me. I hastily decided on the latter, remembering from the detective stories of my boyhood references to 'damning evidence at the scene of the crime'. I wasn't quite sure how the binoculars might constitute evidence, damning or otherwise, but you never *knew* and I wasn't keen to stand about and debate the matter. It proved to be an unfortunate decision.

I picked them up and prepared to go. The quickest way back to the vicarage would have been via the road but by now the morning was unfolding and there would be traffic and people about. To retrace my steps could be equally dangerous: another person in the fields at that hour was unlikely but not impossible, though the presence of bullocks tends to deter dog walkers. It might be a critical choice and of course I dithered. Then sickened by my indecision I turned and started to walk briskly back the way I had come.

There is little of that walk that I recall except that mercifully I met no one and reached home in a state of peculiar calm. Once there I made another pot of tea, smoked a Gold Flake, and with absolutely nothing in my mind sat a long, long time at the kitchen table.

Basil Rummage was due to arrive at six o'clock that evening and eventually I was able to throw off my inertia and direct my thoughts to provisions for his stay and my own departure.

Rummage was not a person I particularly liked. At training college he had been one of the more rumbustious of my fellow ordinands and had combined a quite remarkable obtuseness with an equally remarkable dedication to his own ends. I had no reason to believe that things had changed. A couple of years previously we had encountered each other at a weekend conference, and there too he had displayed both an oafish absurdity and a self-serving cunning. However, that was none of my business. The important thing was that his brief presence here would release me for a well-earned rest and help lend distance to what had just happened.

I went upstairs to pack; checked that the spare bedroom was moderately welcoming, discarded my clerical collar and put on a sports coat. Downstairs I left various notes for Rummage directing him to the larder, the dustbins and the beer. I made no mention of the whisky, assuming (foolishly) that his roving eye would pass over the drinks cabinet. In an access of generosity I left a couple of packets of cigarettes on the kitchen table inviting him to help himself. It was now midday and time to be away from Molehill and en route for my vacation. Leaving the spare key in the pre-arranged place I piled my two small suitcases into the boot of the Singer, backed it out of the garage, narrowly missing a lurking errand-boy, and set its nose for Brighton.

It was, as the earlier signs had promised, the most beautiful day. The Singer though elderly and battered ran smoothly and we were soon out of Surrey and over the border into Sussex. The South Downs reared up distant but comforting and it didn't take long before we were on the old A23

85

Brighton road. The hood was down, the wind gusting and I began to experience a curious exhilaration. The car speeded happily towards the south coast, the Downs looming ever nearer. Soon the Great War Memorial pillars came into sight, were zoomed past, and the outskirts of Brighton appeared. I slowed down appropriately and glided into the Old Staine at a stately pace.

My original intention had been to put up at one of the more salubrious guest houses just off the seafront. For some reason though, I suddenly felt that something better was called for. I am not particularly extravagant but had an unaccustomed urge to indulge myself, to enjoy an accommodation normally beyond my means. I think liberty had a hand in it – though whether the impulse was celebratory or valedictory I cannot be sure. Either way something a little out of the ordinary seemed called for and I decided to try my luck at one of the better hotels. Why not The Old Schooner? It was not quite the best but occupied an excellent position on the seafront and was certainly more fun and smarter than the guest houses lining the lesser streets. I had been in the bar there a couple of times during the war and knew that it had rooms looking out over the promenade and the two piers. What could be better for a summer sojourn?

I parked the car in a side road, went in and enquired. Yes, they had one room left, small but with a little balcony, two floors up and overlooking the sea. I took it immediately and was soon comfortably ensconced.

9

The Vicar's Version

The last time I had been in Brighton was during the war, when there had been rolls of barbed wire along the promenade and the steps to the beach had been removed to frustrate enemy landings. Now, all such impediments were long gone and the shore stretched placid and inviting. I gazed down from the balcony, my eyes sweeping the space between the two piers, taking in the silent scene of splashing children and dogs, paddling women and the few dedicated swimmers. The sun caught the wavelets making them wink and glitter, and far in the distance, remote and toy-like, fishing smacks bobbed serenely. For a few moments I was back in the seaside holidays of my boyhood; and pleasant though it was to watch from afar, the scene beckoned and I wanted to be part of it. I unpacked quickly, took the binoculars I had picked up that morning and went downstairs for a nostalgic walk along the seafront.

It was good to smell the sea air, to feel the sun on the back of my neck and to saunter freely among the other strollers. After a while I decided to venture on to the beach itself – feeling it incumbent upon the dedicated holidaymaker to get as close to the sand and seaweed as possible. (And after all, I mused, the chance might never come again.) As a matter of fact, while seaweed is copious, except when the tide goes far out there is very little sand at Brighton. The beaches on that part of the coast are notoriously pebbly, a condition which some dislike though personally I prefer the discomfort of pebbles to the irritation of gritty sand.

Anyway, entering into the spirit of things I bought a strawberry ice-cream from a kiosk and set off over the crunching shingle until I found a suitable place to sit and finish the now dripping cone. There was a sheltered niche in front of the sea wall where I settled down, took off my shoes and jacket and leant back against the warm stone. The binoculars (rather good ones, I discovered) came in handy, and for ten minutes or so I was engrossed in my surroundings and lazily watched the spectacle of boats and bathers and the comings and goings on the Palace Pier.

The entertainment was interrupted by the arrival of a small Cairn terrier who approached me with a brisk and self-important air, barked a greeting and made a bee-line for my folded jacket. At first, fearing he was about to christen it, I moved to shoo him away but after a few perfunctory sniffs and a couple of tail wags he scampered off to investigate more pressing matters. He was an engaging little fellow and I started to ponder again whether a dog would fit in at the vicarage and my life there. Once I returned to Molehill I would give serious thought to the matter. Meanwhile the sun was making me drowsy, and putting my jacket behind my head I settled back and closed my eyes. Lulled by the cries of seagulls and the distant laughter of children I slipped into a long and dreamless slumber.

When I awoke it was well past five o'clock.

There were shadows on the beach and a sharp breeze had got up. Time to return to the hotel, take a bath, have a drink and then look for a spot of supper. I felt refreshed after my long nap and contemplated the evening with a degree of pleasure. The day's earlier events had all but faded.

Bathed and spruced, I went down to the bar and ordered a large gin and tonic. The room is spacious with wide windows looking out on to the pavement and the sea. It is a venue for visitors and locals alike, and that evening there was a large assorted crowd standing in groups and creating a convivial buzz. I ordered my drink, chose a small table by the wall and sat down with my back against the dark panelling. From here I had a good view of the room and my fellow drinkers. Watching others has always been a source of amusement to me and even as a boy I found it one of the more interesting of spectator sports. It is a good way to pass an idle hour. Ideally one needs an inventive companion but even alone the game of appraisal and speculation makes a diverting pastime.

I took out a cigarette, remembering with a flicker of irritation that I had only matches with me. I enjoy the ceremony of the lighter

– the heaviness in the palm, the snapping open of the cover, the click-clicking of the wheel and the sudden burst of blue flame. It is one of those petty hedonistic rituals which a match doesn't quite fulfil. Given the circumstances, my holiday packing had been a rather abstracted affair and it must have been left on the bed when I was changing my jacket. I reflected grimly that if it was spotted by Rummage he would be as likely to pocket it.

I sipped my drink, listened to the pretensions of some smarmer at the next table, watched a youngish man trying to get off with a sixty-year-old blonde, and debated whether to order dinner in the hotel or go out for something a little more adventurous. Preoccupied with these matters I did not see him at first. When I did I had the shock of my life. It was Nicholas – Nicholas Ingaza, last heard of doing time for importuning at a Turkish bath in Jermyn Street.

He was unmistakable. Older of course, and more lined and gaunt than his forty-five years would normally warrant, but those sardonic blue eyes and graceful, slightly mannered gestures would have identified him anywhere – as indeed they did: here and now. I watched covertly, taking in the thin frame clad in its rather dated chalk-stripe, the sleeked hair brushing his collar, the flashy signet ring. I could even hear – or thought I could – those nasal, vaguely seedy and truculent tones which had set him apart from the rest of us at St Bede's Theological College in those far-off days just after the war.

He must have sensed he was being watched for he suddenly broke off his conversation and shot me a cool heavy-lidded look. I was slightly nonplussed, not knowing whether to acknowledge his presence or affect unawareness. However, the question proved academic for he showed no sign of recognition and turned back to his companion. Feeling relieved though oddly a little disappointed, I attended to my drink and a copy of the evening paper. When I looked up again he had detached himself from his companion and was crossing the room in my direction. Out of the corner of my eye I saw the man at the bar shrug and turn away.

'Well, well, well, Francis Oughterard! Long time, no see. What are *you* doing down here in Brighton all on your owney-oh!' The reedy mocking voice brought back the past with an unsettling jolt.

'I could ask the same, Nicholas,' I replied, drawing up a chair and offering him a cigarette. He made a wry face.

'Oh God, you're not still smoking those awful weeds, are you?' And as if to underline the point he took out his case and withdrew a black Balkan Sobranie, snapped open an enviably slick-looking lighter and settled into his chair, lazily expelling the smoke and sipping some virulent pink mixture in a cocktail glass.

We exchanged a mutual appraisal and engaged in pleasantries describing such aspects of our lives as each was prepared to divulge. I told him a little about Molehill and he told me rather less about his life in Brighton. ('Oh, pictures and such, dear boy...') He asked if I had married and when I said no, grinned and said cryptically, 'Probably as well, there would only have been tears before bedtime.' I was somewhat affronted by that and was about to ask what he meant but thought better of it, and instead directed my attention to his pink drink.

'What ever is it?'

'The Bishop's Floozie,' he answered cheerfully. 'Two parts brandy, one each of Dubonnet and Triple Sec, a dash of angostura and a whisk of rum cream. They make the best ones on the south coast here. You should try one.'

I shuddered. 'No thanks, it sounds disgusting.'

He laughed and then said, 'Talking of bishops, who's yours these days?'

I told him it was Clinker and he almost did the nose trick.

'Good Lord! Horace Clinker. So he's still around! Well, well. Fancy his being your boss – that's a bit of a trial, isn't it?' I agreed that it was just a bit but I could imagine far worse.

'Yes, I daresay. After all, in his heyday old Hor was quite a goer. He and I were on good terms for a while until he met the ghastly Gladys.' He paused a moment and closed his eyes – presumably visualizing the ghastliness. 'And then of course there was that other little problem.' He smirked. 'You may remember.'

'Yes,' I replied drily, 'I remember.' The 'little problem' had in fact been a massive scandal which had rocked St Bede's and almost cost Clinker his promotion. Things of course eventually died down and the righteous public turned its predatory gaze elsewhere. But it had been a close run thing and something which I imagine bishops would not be too keen on recalling.

Nicholas had known Clinker at Oxford in the thirties when the latter was a junior divinity don and Nicholas an undergraduate at Merton reading Classics. I gather they had originally met through some bridge circle, and despite differences in age and background had become close drinking companions. However, Clinker had married, became ordained, and with the advent of war they lost touch completely. What Nicholas had done in the intervening years was unclear, presumably some sort of war service although I didn't recall him mentioning it at college. It was unlikely that he would have been a conscientious objector as being interned for one's principles wasn't exactly Nicholas's style. Anyway, whatever he had been doing, some sort of religious interest must have played a part for when I arrived at St Bede's in late 1946 he was already in his second year.

He was a few years older than me and we didn't have a great deal of contact but I recall being uncomfortably impressed by his air of unctuous anarchy. It happened that Clinker was the then acting Dean and I rather gathered had pulled a few strings to smooth the entry of his old bar crony. Such loyalty was misplaced. For as things turned out the protégé proved a considerable liability. Whereas the influence of Gladys and the requirements of position had resulted in Clinker becoming all but teetotal, Nicholas's consumption had increased prodigiously and he was fast getting the reputation for being a lush. This was not the only reputation he was acquiring. He had developed – or was choosing to indulge – a propensity for close encounters in situations not normally approved.

Clinker had seemed curiously deaf to the rumours, and even the more exotic of Nicholas's adventures passed without obvious comment from the top. In this respect I rather wondered if Nicholas didn't have a bit of a hold over him, something perhaps from their Oxford days which Clinker preferred to let lie. Whatever the reason, Nicholas Ingaza was permitted a wide and louche discretion not usually accorded to trainee vicars – or indeed trainee anythings.

It could not and did not last. The drunken escapades and dubious trips to the West End culminated in a midnight telephone call from the police. There followed inevitably the usual lurid court case in all its prurience. Embarrassment fell in every direction. Publicly the college attracted its fair share of sniggering curiosity while privately Clinker was reprimanded for his laxity and ill-placed sponsorship. Matters were tense for him. Yet somehow despite all the fuss with the Church authorities he managed to maintain his position, rising in fact with surprising speed to his present episcopal status. Even the Turkish baths where Nicholas executed his dastardly gaffe continued to flourish, and indeed gained a fashionable notoriety. Only the culprit really suffered: ejected from the college, carted off to clink, and never heard of again until that evening in the summer of 1957 in the lounge bar of The Old Schooner, Brighton.

Our conversation turned to less delicate matters and I told him a little more about Molehill, its mellow twelfth-century church and the more recherché tombs in its rambling graveyard.

'Your parish sounds a straight run,' he observed. 'Trust you to wangle a cushy number. Though apparently you did get a bit pious and energetic for a time; really pulled the wool over their lordships' eyes. All that "muscular" Christianity!' He giggled, adding, 'But it cost you, didn't it, old man. Couldn't stand the pace, I heard.' I was nettled by these remarks and said coldly that I didn't know what he meant.

'Had a little upset, didn't you? So I gathered.'

'I did not have an upset!' I exclaimed irritably. 'I merely got rather tired, that's all.' He had always been tiresome.

'Well, I suppose that's one way of describing it.'

'At least I didn't get thrown out from anywhere!' I retorted.

'That's true, Francis,' he said thoughtfully. 'You always did manage to keep your head above water. Dark horses have a habit of walking just on the safe side – if you'll excuse the yoking of metaphors.' And he smiled sardonically. Bugger the metaphors, I thought. Some safe side! However, I laughed in return, made a breezy comment and steered the conversation elsewhere. I did not care for the direction it was taking.

To ease the mood I asked about Clinker in the old days: had he really been as human as Nicholas implied?

'Oh yes!' he exclaimed. 'Once upon a time Clinker was really quite bright – in both senses of the word. He had a certain intelligence – which of course became clouded after meeting Gladys – and a sense of humour too, albeit of a rather bald kind. He also had a penchant for strong cocktails.' He saw the sceptical look on my face, and went on, 'Yes – gin in various guises, though his particular downfall was White Ladies. They used to be thought rather a feminine tipple but Hor took to the mix like a duck to water. Couldn't get enough of the stuff. There was one frightful occasion when...' He broke off, gave a humourless smile and said, 'Then of course Gladys came on the scene. She soon put a stop to that – and quite a lot of other things too.' For a brief moment he looked almost wistful, and then roared with what I felt was slightly forced laughter.

We chatted on casually for a while, recalling former colleagues, but the conversation grew desultory. Too much water had passed under our bridges; that and a certain mutual wariness made intimacy impossible.

Finally he stood up and announced his departure: 'Well, Francis, I wish you all good luck in your Molehill. Here's my number in the unlikely event you should ever want it. Give my regards to the good bishop when next you see him. Time I was off. Have to see a man about, er...' and he paused mockingly, 'something or other – you know.' I didn't know and didn't care to.

Touching his hair lightly he moved towards the swing-doors where he turned, winked slowly and broadly, and with a languid wave disappeared into the passage and, as I then thought, once more out of my life. I decided to dine in after all.

10

The Cat's Memoir

Having satisfied myself that St Botolph's graveyard was indeed the paradise that it had first seemed, my investigations were now complete. The vicarage itself was less utopian, but being a creature of eminent reasonableness I understand the virtue of compromise and – when it suits me – can practise it. I had intended to make a closer scrutiny of the vicar but was thwarted by his unexpected absence.

Peering in at the window I saw in his place a rather questionable type sprawled at the kitchen table. Since he was wearing a dog collar (not my favourite term) I took him to be one of F.O.'s associates. There was an array of bottles in front of him and two or three copies of *Sporting Life*. I am not enamoured of horses – they would kick a cat as soon as look at it – so was not impressed with the visitor's choice of reading. However, it was imperative that I got my paws under the table, and so without more ado I jumped boldly through the open window ready to make soft-soapy overtures. You may recall that my previous attempts with Flirty-Gerty had not been a success, but she of course was a feeble Pom and I expected better results this time.

All went according to plan. The man (whose name I later learned to be Rummage), although patently a loon, was nevertheless susceptible to my blandishments. I purred cosily in what Bouncer would call a 'matey way' and rubbed my back endearingly around his ankles. These of course were just the preliminaries, softening-up tactics. My *coup de théâtre* was to follow. One of the chief things I have learned about human beings is that they love to be amused. If you can make them laugh then you are more than halfway to success.

Thus I commenced my circus tricks: a couple of balletic leaps, much chasing of tail, three brilliantly executed steps on my hind legs, and then a graceful sinking down upon my back with legs waving languidly and furry tummy displayed for tickling. They can't resist it. And nor did Rummage. He started to make all the usual responses, flattered to think that he had been selected for special attention (as indeed he had), and soon a bowl of milk appeared followed by some not unpleasant pilchards.

These I consumed, sang again for my supper by indulging in a few more absurd antics, and then curled up discreetly behind the sofa in the sitting room. Two days later, as far as Rummage was concerned I was part of the household and he had got into the habit of putting out saucers of milk and fish. I just hoped that F.O. would have the courtesy to continue the practice when he returned from wherever he had gone.

11

The Vicar's Version

I did not sleep as well as I had expected and experienced long periods of wakefulness punctuated by dreams of a disturbing and bizarre nature. The most memorable of these seemed to involve Nicholas and Elizabeth engaged in a convoluted foxtrot in the ballroom of the Blackpool Tower while I, sporting a bishop's mitre if you please, endeavoured to keep the band in some semblance of tune. Somewhere from the region of the tearooms I kept hearing the bark of a rutting roebuck. It was all very wearing and I awoke at seven o'clock the next morning feeling tired and bleak. The weather had changed overnight, and instead of the previous day's bright sunshine there was now a surly mist greying the windows and generally blighting the spirit. I lay staring at the ceiling contemplating the future and God knows what.

The immediate future was of course my sister Primrose and her new house between Brighton and Lewes. She had moved in four days previously and I liked to think that by the time I arrived the more arduous tasks would have been addressed by the removal men and kindly neighbours. I saw my own role as being supportive rather than practical.

I quite like my sister, and having observed other people's consider myself lucky in having one who is relatively undemanding. Primrose is five years older than me; and like me tall, thin and unmarried. I don't know why this last should be – women tend to marry on the whole – but it may be something to do with her monumental selfishness. I don't mean selfish in the sense of being mean-spirited or unpleasant – nothing as obvious or paltry as that – but rather a total absorption in her own world and requirements. Provided that world is not impinged upon nor those requirements thwarted, Primrose is the model of civilized decency. But on the rare occasions when liberties are taken and boundaries crossed her capacity for resentment is prodigious and she assumes an energy for prejudice which, speaking as one who tires easily, I find remarkable.

The other outlet for Primrose's energy is her painting at which she is surprisingly good. I say 'surprisingly' because one never really expects a member of one's own family to be especially talented at anything; competent perhaps, but hardly *good*. Indeed, I recall our parents being distinctly put out when as a young woman Primrose began to display her quite exceptional (for our circle) artistic skills, and it was with a grudging and embarrassed grace that they were prevailed upon to send their daughter to the Courtauld Institute. Here it was intended she spend her days studying the Old Masters and honing her talent. She must have done a bit of that, I suppose; but from what I recollect – and subsequently heard – she passed much of her time engaged in subtle but dedicated riot – in which masters, both old and young, seemed to play a substantial part. Curiously Primrose's florid lifestyle never really reflected itself in her pictures, for her particular and lucrative forte is the depiction of Sussex scenes – mainly Downland churches and grimly po-faced sheep; a choice of subject baffling to those who confidently expect to see a painter's life mirrored in their art.

Anyway, there were three full days at my disposal before the visit to Primrose and her new house. The sea mist was clearing and already hints of sun had started to appear. I thought I would begin the time by re-acquainting myself with the Royal Pavilion and exploring the older parts of Brighton. On one of the days a jaunt over the Downs would be nice, motoring to Birling Gap and the Seven Sisters, even perhaps as far as the old Belle Tout lighthouse at Beachy Head. I enjoy such meanderings and the prospect of sea air and freedom was pleasing.

In the meantime should I book a trip around the two piers on one of those sleek speedboats which the more intrepid trippers were queuing for? However, as I looked more closely at the motion of the craft and the rearing and slapping of its prow, I doubted whether my rather delicate stomach could cope. Regretfully I decided against it – one of the chugging motor launches was probably more my style. I was carrying Elizabeth's binoculars and it also occurred to me that it would be a shame not to put them to good use, so perhaps a visit to Plumpton race-course might be arranged or even over to Goodwood. The possibilities were numerous! First though to the Pavilion and the charms of Mrs Fitzherbert's yellow drawing room.

Having had only a light breakfast, by noon I was feeling quite peckish, and after the perambulations amidst the Prince Regent's chinoiserie was in need of a mild bracer. There was a small and ancient-looking pub down a side street and I went in and ordered some ham sandwiches and a glass of beer. I don't normally like beer but felt thirsty and it seemed in any case somehow appropriate to the holiday mood. There were only a few other drinkers huddled in corners, and the place was dark, quiet and restfully non-descript. I sipped my drink and contemplated the dartboard, and for some reason an expert player I had once admired came into my mind: a WAAF called Madge.

During the war I had been on leave in the town a couple of times. It was hardly a safe haven – that stretch of coast attracting returning enemy bombers like moths to a candle – but it had been fun all the same. The place had been swarming with Forces personnel, particularly the RAF from Tangmere, and included the usual bevy of female auxiliaries, many of them Wrens billeted at Roedean. I could never achieve that ease with girls which came so naturally to most of my colleagues. It wasn't that I shunned their company, but I could not entirely breach that careless circle of brazen joke and knowing laughter, and hovered diffidently on its edge envious of my friends and fearful of my own shyness. Somehow I knew that their sprawling world of easy and insouciant sex would never belong to me, would never really open its doors. Except that it did, just once, just fleetingly – through the ministrations of Madge Rivers.

Madge was what used to be known as a 'goer' – racy, disgraceful, delightful; and she was kind-hearted. Indeed her kind heart amounted to an almost missionary zeal, and on three sunlit afternoons in the confines of a boarding-house bedroom she instructed me carefully and cheerfully in the 'man–woman relationship'. The experience was not unpleasant but it was more tiring and certainly more complicated than I had hitherto imagined. Madge applied herself with infinite patience and appalling humour. Feet stuck high in the air (principally I suspect to admire her scarlet toenails), she would giggle her instructions while I pushed and fumbled between her ample thighs. Then, spurred on by her yelps of encouragement, I would eventually reach where I was supposed to be and collapse on top of her in a grateful heap. After a while I too learnt to laugh, and as I turned lazily on my back would glimpse from between the half-drawn curtains some of that dazzling sun which must have been making her toes glint...

I finished my beer and went over to the shadowy bar and bought the other half. Back in my seat I mentally toasted Madge and thought ruefully that probably by now she was fat with five children and living in Penge. I hoped not – she deserved better. Perhaps, I brightened, she was the madam of a high-class brothel in Mayfair boosting the morale, and other things, of tyro punters. To that pious hope I raised my glass.

I don't often think of women and I suppose it was that which, with a dreadful lurch, brought Elizabeth Fotherington back into my mind. Not that there was the remotest similarity between mentor and tormentor, but perhaps it was the unaccustomed musing on an individual person that made me recall Elizabeth and the events surrounding her unfortunate demise. It was the first time I had had either the leisure or the inclination to analyse the details of the matter or indeed give real thought to future action. For a few lurid minutes I relived that encounter in the woods, recalling the resinous mossy smell, the pheasants, the stillness, the distant barking. I also recalled *her* rearing up, breathless and beaming amidst those innocent branches... I closed my eyes.

What I couldn't make out was why she had been there at all – and what about the binoculars? Why on earth was she toting those around with her at that early hour? Did she nurse an 'undying passion' for birds as well as tulips? Had the morning beckoned her irresistibly to seek magnified sightings of thrush and skylark or other woodland prey? I didn't know ... and then of course I did!

Prey. That was it! *I* had been the prey, was

being stalked that June morning and my movements followed obsessively through the lenses of her glasses. She must have had them trained on the vicarage from the upper windows of her house, had seen me leave in the direction of the wood; and then, rushing through the garden and out by the wicket gate (that 'postern of fate'), had cut through the furze and brambles to the main path – and to me, her unwitting victim, idling along minding my own empty business.

Grotesque though the idea was, it had a sort of dreadful irony and would certainly account for her dishevelled state and short-ness of breath. Despite the horror of it all I found myself grinning with incredulity. To think that I of all people should have been singled out as the quarry for such insatiable desire! It had a certain piquancy all right: yet another of God's practical jokes leading to dire consequences. The world had a surfeit of such comedy.

The rest of my time in Brighton was spent pleasantly enough, but memories of Eliza-beth had started to cast their long shadow and I could not quite recapture that holiday ease which had first coloured my hours in the town. Thus I shelved the idea of going to the races, the binoculars by now having lost their novelty and indeed become distinctly irksome. I looked forward to my sojourn with Primrose, trusting that fresh diversions would lift the spirit and stiffen the mind for whatever might lie ahead.

I arrived there at six o'clock in the evening. She greeted me with her customary mix of distant affection and quizzical amusement; informed me that my hair was going grey and that I looked even thinner than usual. The first I knew, the other did not surprise me. She offered to show me the two chinchilla rabbits she had recently acquired, Boris and Karloff, but I told her they must wait while I took sustenance of her gin.

'Haven't got any,' she said with a note of relish. 'Only my usual dry sherry.' I winced. Primrose's sherry was invariably South African and of a brand so desiccated that to call it bone dry would have been a kindness. However, steeling both nerve and palate I accepted a glass and embarked on a leisurely tour of her new abode.

She had chosen well. The house was of 1920s design: solid, roomy and mainly south-facing. There were four bedrooms of which one had a skylight, and with its high ceiling and airy proportions it would be ideal as a studio. It could also accommodate her accumulated stocks of church and sheep sketches. From the small veranda overlooking the garden one could see the bold and treeless curve of the Downs. The garden itself was full of trees and I noticed apprehensively that though attractive it was severely overgrown. I rather suspected it would be my task to set it to rights. It was.

Primrose does not cook; she assembles. Nevertheless, the assemblage is unfailingly deft and well chosen (an influence from her Courtauld days?) and supper that evening had, by my limited standards, the quality of a feast. It was a feast, however, slightly compromised by the remarks with which she prefaced it.

We were in the kitchen: me struggling with the corkscrew while she carved slices of ham and thick chunks of French sausage (contraband from Dieppe). Apropos of nothing she suddenly said, 'It's very odd, that murder business, you know. I hope it doesn't involve you in any way.' My hand slipped and I broke the cork. Staring fixedly at its brown flecks scattered over the draining board I enquired what murder she was referring to.

'The one in your parish of course. It was all in yesterday's *Argus*: some old trout

112

found strangled in the woods. From what I can make out quite near to your vicarage. It says she was done in on Tuesday afternoon.'

I was about to say, 'Tuesday morning actually,' but instead muttered vaguely that it must have happened after I had left for Brighton, and why in any case did she think it would involve me.

'It says she used to attend St Botolph's church – that's the name of yours, isn't it? And after all, Francis, you do have a knack of getting embroiled in things.'

'I do not!' I protested indignantly. 'What *are* you talking about?'

'Don't you remember when the milkman paid you five guineas to do his rounds for him while he went to bed with the doctor's wife? There was an awful stink and Daddy was so cross!'

'But that was years ago, I was just a boy!' I exclaimed.

'Old enough to keep all the money to yourself and give none to your penniless sister toiling at art school,' she retorted tartly, spearing one of the sausage bits. I recollected that my meanness with the spoils had indeed rankled with her – as it evidently still did. Primrose has an acute sense of injustice where her own interests are concerned.

113

'And what about that arsenal you almost blew up on the Isle of Wight? They nearly cashiered you for that.'

'Well, that was hardly my fault,' I began defensively, 'it was Billings, he–'

'Perhaps not. But just think of that ghastly business at the seminary place you were in. Splashed all over the newspapers, it was. I thought Mother was going to die of apoplexy. And it was so tiresome as I was expected to stay and look after her.'

She took the bottle from me, gouged out the rest of the cork, poured herself a large glass and as an afterthought filled a lesser one for me. 'I am not saying you had anything to do with it, but you were *there*, and it did make waves... I mean completely ruined my chances with the editor of the *Sunday Noise*. Once he knew I had a brother at that place all he wanted was one thing, and one thing only: inside information. The bed never got a look in!'

I could see that that too rankled and began to feel apologetic. She must have noticed my discomfort for in milder tones she said, 'Anyway, regarding this murder of yours – if the press approach you looking for special angles, local colour or whatever it is they always want, just don't mention your artist sister in Sussex. I don't want hordes of reporters and bishops swarming down here!'

'Why bishops?' I enquired.

'My dear, they get in everywhere. Don't you remember the St Bede's thing?'

Personally I could think of only one bishop in evidence at that time, Clinker's superior, Boxwick. However, during the scandal his views and photograph had appeared with such daily monotony that I assumed Primrose had mistaken the one for the many. I refrained from telling her, not wishing to stir further contention. The matter was shelved and we turned to the more pressing issues of the garden and the chinchillas.

12

The Vicar's Version

When I got back to Molehill I saw that Rummage had done his worst. The vicarage was a minor shambles, especially the kitchen where empty beer bottles competed with unwashed plates for space on the small draining board. The waste bin overflowed with mouldering corned beef tins, discarded cigarette packets and screwed-up copies of the *Daily Sketch*. Around its base was a confetti of shredded betting slips. (Anyone would think we were RCs, I thought irritably) Needless to say my lighter was nowhere to be seen. After unpacking and putting things to right I went to the bathroom where I discovered a note propped on the windowsill. Why there I do not know but the mind of Rummage moves in mysterious ways. It read as follows:

Dear Oughterard,

Nice little place you've got here. Hope you enjoyed the briny etc. etc. Have dented your gatepost but expect you can mend it all right. Some old girl was found dead in the wood and a couple of heavies turned up on the doorstep asking for you. Told them you'd be back soon and they went off quite happily mumbling something about routine enquiries. Let me know if you want me again.

B.R.

P.S. I like your cat.

Looking back, I am not sure which part of the note rattled me most: the news of the police visit or the reference to the cat (the gatepost bit being no more than expected from Rummage). I knew of course from the item in the *Brighton Argus* which Primrose had shown me that the police were already on to it, and had also guessed that since the victim was one of my congregation I could expect to be approached for details concerning her social or even personal life. However, it was one thing to recognize the probability and quite another to have it so baldly confirmed in Rummage's unkempt scrawl. What had been a distant and theoretical prospect suddenly took on an alarming and imminent reality. But I was also puzzled by the allusion to the non-existent cat. Had Rummage suffered an hallucination? If so perhaps he had also mistaken the visit from the police. For about five seconds I clung to this comforting thought but it was hardly a hope I could sustain.

As in all times of tension I went downstairs to put the kettle on and lit a cigarette. Poised for my second puff, I suddenly sensed a presence at the window and had an uncanny feeling of déjà vu. For a wild instant I was gripped by a spasm of desperate panic. Then slowly putting down my cigarette and taking a deep breath I shot a furtive glance and saw,

117

not the resurrected bane of my life but ... her Creature. Maurice's querulous face was squashed against the pane, the flattened nose and splayed whiskers suggesting some feline invention of Hieronymus Bosch. Just as Nicholas had been unmistakable so was Maurice. The unusual markings and accusing stare could have belonged only to him.

We confronted each other through the glass and despite my vague hand-flappings it was obvious he had no intention of deserting his perch. After a little I cautiously opened the side window and he snaked along the ledge and slipped through. Once inside he stalked around imperiously, taking not a blind bit of notice of me, and then walked purposefully into the sitting room where he settled down behind the sofa. He seemed remarkably well orientated and I assumed this was the mythical cat which had endeared itself to Rummage. I doubted whether he would do the same for me.

The cat's invasion was an irritant but of minor concern compared to the weightier matters I should soon have to confront. Brighton and my sister's house had been a therapy, a diversionary respite; but now I was home again and on the brink of heaven knew what dire eventualities! I re-read Rummage's note. Yes, without a doubt *They* would be back. On any day, at any hour. I glanced out of the window half expecting to see dark-helmeted figures lumbering up the front path, handcuffs in hand, whistles at the ready... Nothing. The garden with its gaunt buddleia and etiolated roses returned my gaze with a still and blank indifference.

After a scratch supper I went into the study to attack the post. Rummage had been uncharacteristically useful in piling it up neatly on the top of my desk. There were the usual bills, church circulars, notices of diocese meetings, jumble sales etc., two indecipherable postcards from an aunt in Calais or Timbuktu – and a long manila envelope neatly typed and postmarked London WC1. On the back in italic script was engraved the name *Messrs Switcher, Switcher & Pang, of Bedford Row*. This meant nothing to me and having disposed of the other detritus I slit open the envelope. The letter was brief and to the point:

Dear Sir,

Re: The Will of the late Mrs Elizabeth Fotherington of Marchbank House, Molehill, Surrey

We are pleased to inform you that under the terms of the codicil attached to the above mentioned will you are to receive the sum of £25,000 (twenty five thousand pounds). Please be so good as to sign and send the enclosed form acknowledging receipt of this letter after which the said monies can be released to you once probate has been established.

Yours faithfully, etc., etc.

I stared down at the words in a state of dumb incredulity. They were gross, inexplicable, crazy ... marvellous. For a few seconds I was gripped with a mad euphoria – what couldn't I do with £25,000! (Approximately £400,000 purchase power by today's values.) On reflection, not a great deal really. My pleasures are of a mainly sedentary kind. Sport and travel I find tiring, and apart from a long-held hankering for a rod on the Test I harboured few adventurous dreams. It did, however, strike me that here at last would be the chance to hire a first rate piano teacher to steer me through the labyrinth of the *Goldberg Variations* – or indeed the exquisite syncopations of Teddy Wilson. But apart from the music and the fishing it seemed that I might be hard pressed to do justice to my good fortune. Still, £25,000 was a reassuring prospect and for a brief while I was lost in a reverie of happy speculation.

Naturally it did not last. The ghastly irony hit me, and with the irony came guilt – but a guilt soon overlaid by blinding panic. *Here* was the motive, for Christ's sake! All this time I had felt moderately safe in the assumption that there was absolutely nothing to connect me with what had happened; there was no reason (none that any sane person might imagine) that would prompt me, a quiet ineffectual parson, to do away with the foolish Mrs Fotherington. *Now*, here I was down in black and white as a substantial beneficiary under her will; my name linked irrevocably with hers. It was dreadful, it was too bad. It was typical of that bloody woman! All the old despairs and fears came flooding back, and engulfed by a sudden wave of vertigo I sat on the floor and wept in horrified anguish.

After a while, ashamed of my craven collapse I got up, went into the sitting room and sat down at the piano. I lifted my hands but when they came down it was no melody they performed, but scales. Slow at first, desultory; but gradually the repetitive movement took control and the energy flowed. Relentlessly my fingers made their obsessive assault on the keys. Up and down, up and down, up and down ... my hands flew swiftly, adroitly over their familiar course until eventually, steadied by the sheer mechanics of the exercise, I felt a returning poise and, strangely, an almost light-headed indifference.

Closing the lid I remembered the cat. Last seen he had been ensconced behind the sofa. I peered over the back, and sure enough there was the sleek dark bundle apparently fast asleep. Certainly the eyes were tightly shut – though as I was later to learn of Maurice that does not necessarily signify sleep or oblivion.

Calmed by my bout at the piano I felt sufficiently confident to make some further acquaintance, and bending down scooped the creature up and carried him into the kitchen. He looked askance and struggled furiously but resolution was upon me and I told him firmly that if he wanted to remain in the house and get anything to eat then he had better damn well co-operate. As I was also later to learn, the concept of cooperation is alien to Maurice. However, that evening he did seem to recognize that at least a show of reasonableness would be in his interests and augur well for his future welfare. Thus we effected a relationship of fragile deference which remains moderately intact to the present day.

13

The Vicar's Version

The next morning I sat at my desk catching up on a plethora of neglected paperwork: the Boiler Fund Appeal, altar-boy lists, the byzantine reports of the Vestry Circle – matters which I generally find less than absorbing; but that day their very dullness induced a sense of security and I applied myself with unusual zeal. Indeed so immersed was I that the wretched bequest was all but forgotten, and it was nearly one o'clock when I put down my fountain pen and looked with satisfaction at the piles of completed documents stacked neatly on the window-sill. Time for a gin and a breather.

Time also to check the church and inspect the new hassocks and candlesticks delivered in my absence. I strolled up the lane connecting the church with the vicarage. In the distance a stout tweed-clad figure was marching through the lychgate: Miss Dalrymple, doyenne of the hymn book menders and scourge of choirboys.

There must be few people who make it their regular mission in life to crawl on all-fours between the lines of choir stalls circling with a stick of chalk the wads of chewing-gum deposited on their undersides. However, such a one was Miss Dalrymple. Given the awkwardness of the manoeuvre, she executed it with remarkable skill – of a kind normally associated with circus contortionists and presumably the result of years of experience and a cussed dedication to the pursuit of small boys. These latter, confronted with the chalk-marked fruits of their wrongdoing, would be required to prise off the offending bits with tins of Vim and wire-wool: a laborious monthly ritual which I took care to distance myself from, feeling in any case that Miss Dalrymple's powers of coercion were vastly superior to mine.

She hailed me cheerfully, said she hoped I had had a good holiday and did I know that poor Mrs Fotherington had met a 'too dreadful end in that awful wood'. Just why the wood should be so designated was not clear, and I was about to say that I had always found it rather peaceful and attractive but stopped quickly. The less knowledge displayed about that particular area the better. Despite the sympathetic words I detected a gleam of excitement in her eye and reflected that to one less intimately involved the event might indeed hold a certain ghoulish appeal. All right for some, I thought glumly.

'It's good to have you back,' she said benignly. 'At last things can be put on an even keel again' – meaning presumably that she and the rest of the congregation could continue to do just as they had always done with no undue interruption from their pastor. 'Your locum, the Reverend Rummage, was very nice but just a trifle overbearing, you know.' I did know. 'Though I must say,' she added, 'his departing sermon was one of the most rousing I have ever heard! We were most impressed.'

'Really?' I said curiously. 'What was his theme?'

'Self-denial and the ordered life.' I thought of the shambles in my kitchen and his dastardly raid on the malt whisky.

'Ah yes, very imaginative, the Reverend Rummage...'

She took her leave and I went into the church where I busied myself with rearranging the candlesticks, admiring the new designs of the hassocks, checking the security lights and saying a few words to the cleaners. I like pottering in the church. It is a soothing, mildly aesthetic experience; and occasionally if there is nobody about I will have a crafty go on the organ. I say 'crafty' because I am embarrassed by my conspicuous lack of expertise (being much more secure on the piano), but also because the organist regards the instrument as his personal property and turns nasty should anyone have the temerity to approach it. However, that afternoon was not the time for such adventures and I did not linger, hoping instead to draft a couple of sermons before Evensong and ponder my response to the police when they came – as come they surely would.

On my way back I encountered Reginald Bowler. He did not have his dog with him and looked morose. I smiled politely, expecting some passing rebuff, but he stopped full in my path and in a cold voice said, 'So you're back, are you? Returned to enjoy the spoils, I suppose.'

'Er – I am not sure if I understand...' I began in some confusion.

'Of course you do, man. That money she left you!' He glared ferociously

'Whoever told you that?' I exclaimed.

'Her daughter, Violet Pond.'

'Violet *what?*'

'Pond,' he spluttered. 'Didn't you hear me? Pond! Pond!'

I stepped back hastily, trying to dodge the cascade of spray, and in so doing experienced a sudden flash of vivid memory: the last time it had been necessary to side-step Bowler the awful fracas with the dog had ensued. This time my foot met no such solid object. But Bowler was solid all right – solidly close, and impossible!

I said coolly that I had no idea who this daughter was and certainly did not understand why she should be discussing my bequest with him. He raised his eyes to the heavens. 'Because I am the co-executor of course. I know about these things! Not that I knew anything about that absurd codicil ... only inserted a few days before she died. It made a hell of a difference. She should have had the whole thing dealt with here at the bank under *my* vigilance instead of traipsing up to London and depositing it with those wide-boy solicitors. Meddling bunch! She made other changes too. Mrs Pond is getting considerably less than she banked on – a nice bit of course – but she's none too pleased all the same. And do you know what she left me?' Before I could hazard a guess he went crashing on, 'A measly one hundred pounds – a *hundred pounds* if you please! After all I did for her! And *you* waltz off with God knows how much... I tell you it's a disgrace, a disgrace, sir!'

As he ranted I wondered whether I should murmur something helpful about heavenly riches or camels and needles, but thought better of it. In his present state such reminders might not be entirely welcome. He certainly looked a funny colour and was perspiring heavily (As a matter of fact I did not feel too good myself. The news that the codicil had been added only days before her death fuelled my earlier fears and already I could see the finger of suspicion hovering perilously near.) Instead I said I was sorry that he felt so upset but there was really nothing I could do about it and I was sure Mrs Fotherington had always valued his friendship. This struck me as a fairly reasonable response in the circumstances but it seemed to inflame him further.

'Well, don't imagine you are going to bury her as well,' he snapped. 'As soon as the pathologist released the body the daughter had the whole caboosh conducted in St Elspeth's in Guildford. The family was in its parish for years and still have strong links. They do things properly there. So *your* services will not be required, vicar.'

This was the first good news I had had all day. Nevertheless, I was stung by the aspersion cast on my handling of the Burial Service. This is something in which I have always taken particular pride, conducting the obsequies with a combination of gravitas and polish rare among the minor clergy – in whose ranks I naturally count myself.

'What's more,' he went on, 'I think you will find that Violet Pond intends to contest the will. She's decidedly miffed about your part in it – as well she might be. You'll be hearing from her, I fancy.' With that as his parting shot he turned abruptly and stalked off in the direction whence he had come. I could not help wondering where it was he had been going in the first place – presumably a destination of little account. I watched him disappear, pondering that final remark. Surely, having disposed of the mother, I was not now going to be plagued by the daughter as well!

14

The Cat's Memoir

I had been sunning myself on top of one of my favourite tombstones when there was a crashing in the bushes. Bouncer stood there. Rather to my surprise I noticed he was toting his mangy rubber ring. Normally he left his toys behind when visiting or pounding the block with Bowler (except I recall when he caught me, in that humiliating contretemps with the Veasey women). He looked a little seedy – even, one might say, hangdog. Dropping the ring he sat down heavily on his haunches and peered up through the matted fronds of his fringe.

'He's gone off,' he announced.

'Gone off?' I queried. 'You mean Bowler has gone down to Worthing to stay with that noisome sister of his?'

'No,' he said testily 'South America.'

'Nonsense,' I rejoined briskly 'You've got it wrong. What on earth would Bowler be doing in South America?'

'Hiding from the police. He's snaffled the dough from the bank, filled his pockets and done a runner.'

Bouncer's crude mode of speech has long been a source of irritation to me, so I enunciated my reply carefully: 'You mean your master has appropriated the funds and absconded.'

'Yes, that's what I said – the bastard's scarpered and left me behind.'

I winced at this travesty of my words but it was clearly not the time to dispute linguistic niceties. Instead I gazed at him, taking in the full import of the news, and then ventured to enquire, 'So where does that leave you?'

'In the doghouse,' he growled, shoving his rubber ring around with his paw.

There was a long silence as we both contemplated the implications of this. As such places go I gather the local Dogs' Home is not so bad; raucous of course – then you would expect that from a largely vagrant population – but I hear the treatment is quite good and that it also provides a kennel facility for dogs whose owners are temporarily absent. But now to all intents and purposes Bouncer had no owner. And even if the errant Bowler returned he would presumably be in no position to reclaim his lost property. The idea of Bouncer being farmed out to a set of total strangers (or something worse) was a prospect I found oddly disturbing. Fortunately I have a fertile brain, and a plan immediately presented itself.

'You could move in here,' I said. 'It's quite nice really. The vicar's a bit clumsy and crashes around on the piano keys but by and large he is fairly innocuous. Ponces about in his surplice now and again but you get used to that.'

'What's *nockus?*' Bouncer asked.

'It means harmless,' I explained kindly. He said nothing but a quizzical faraway look came into his eyes, and then he burped loudly.

I ignored that and continued, 'The only drawback is those confounded bells. One could hardly hear them in The Avenue but here they make an infernal noise!'

'Oh, I like the sound of bells – they speak to a fellow's soul,' he said solemnly.

Despite the grimness of the situation I was assailed by a spasm of mirth which I contrived to contain by a sudden bout of sneezing. The idea of Bouncer possessing a soul, let alone one receptive to the cacophony of church bells, was something that I had never really considered. It just went to show that there must be something concealed in those doggy depths after all! 'Well, that's all right then,' I said quickly. 'We had better get you billeted.'

Obviously it would not be possible for Bouncer to get into the vicarage immediately. Vague though he is, even F.O. might notice a strange dog suddenly wandering about his house or rolling on the sofa. I felt that Bouncer should be introduced in stages so that the vicar could become acclimatized to his presence. To this end I suggested that for an interim period Bouncer could use the church crypt for his sleeping arrangements and then during the day make fleeting appearances in the garden.

The crypt looked a bit damp and toady and I was not sure how he would react to the proposal. However, he seemed more than happy, and dragging his ring padded down the crumbling steps and disappeared through the broken panel in the door. I hovered about a little, not sure whether he expected me to accompany him. I was not particularly disposed to as I knew from bitter experience that the resident mice were less than couth. Fortunately he soon reappeared and from the vigorous tail wagging I assumed that things had met with his approval.

'I say,' he said, 'I know a good joke about cats and crypts! Shall I tell it to you? It's a tongue-twister. It goes like this: "The cat crept into the crypt, cra–"'

'Yes,' I said hastily. 'We all know that one. Very funny, I'm sure. Remember where you are. It's hardly the place for coarseness of that kind.' He seemed quite unabashed and scampered around in a circle snorting loudly. For one who had just lost his master to the wiles of avarice he seemed to have recovered remarkably quickly. Still, I suppose that in the grip of severe shock even the best of dogs can become crude and facetious, and Bouncer I fear is not of the best.

'It's a bit of all right down there,' he said. 'There's only one problem – I've left a few valuables back at home.' I had visited his home on a number of occasions when his master was out, and having encountered Bouncer's basket had a good idea what those 'valuables' might be. The basket was far from pretty, and its contents – articles which I preferred not to view too closely – even less so. Old, chewed, hairy, they did not present an edifying sight. Presumably these were the things he was hankering after.

'You still have your nice rubber ring,' I said encouragingly.

'Dogs do not live by rubber rings alone,' he answered tartly.

Even I could find no response to that and resigned myself to the task of helping him retrieve the valuables.

We embarked on the rescue venture that evening, having spent a pleasant afternoon roaming the graveyard. I enjoyed giving Bouncer a conducted tour, showing him the finer points and facilities and generally airing my knowledge of its more esoteric aspects. He was clearly impressed but did take an unconscionable time christening the boundaries of his new territory. You would have thought that having deposited his marker in one place it would be unnecessary to return to the identical spot quite so often. He explained that he had been brought up to be thorough – a claim that I rather doubted.

Getting to Bowler's house was easy: down the lane, over the vet's stile, past the Veaseys' fishpond, and then via a back alley into Bowler's kitchen garden. Getting back with all of Bouncer's impedimenta was a different matter. It took each of us several journeys and I have known few things more fatiguing. However, to give Bouncer his due he was properly appreciative of my efforts, and to celebrate our success we feasted on some bits of chicken liberated from F.O.'s pantry.

As things turned out it was just as well that we went when we did. Despite the lateness of the hour we were surprised on letting ourselves in through the dog-flap to find a *police presence*. In the lounge there was a detective constable of about fourteen holding a glass of Bowler's whisky in one hand and picking his nose with the other. In the hall a beefy female sergeant was bellowing down the telephone:

'Yes, yes, sir ... we're leaving now. We've found those files you wanted plus the Buenos Aires addresses... That sister from Worthing has been on the blower again. She might be useful but at the moment all she can do is burble on about some bloody dog. Says she'll have it put down given half a chance. God Almighty, I'll have her put down if she doesn't shut up and co-operate. These damn people, they never seem to realize...'

I noticed that Bouncer had gone a little pale around the chops, and quickly hustled him out into the garden. Here we crouched among the vegetable marrows until the lights went out and the coast was clear. Then sneaking back into the house we started to gather up his toys and trophies. Fortunately this was an exacting task and helped to keep his mind off the threats from Worthing.

Our labours finally completed and F.O.'s chicken demolished, I left him to drag his baggage down to the crypt and retired for a couple of hours' rest before commencing my nightly prowl. This was productive and I returned pleasantly refreshed. Passing the crypt I paused at the top of the steps wondering how Bouncer was getting on. From the depths there emanated a fur-raising noise: a sort of strangulated howling whose volume and pitch fluctuated in the most uncanny way moving from a deep throaty bass to a high falsetto wail. Fortunately I had heard a little of this on other occasions, otherwise despite my undoubted fortitude I might have been severely alarmed. It was in fact merely Bouncer running through his baying scales. Nevertheless, I was struck by the sheer variety of the ululations, and it was certainly a sound to wake the dead, as – I reflected – it was quite probably doing.

The next morning I lurked about waiting for him to surface which he eventually did looking even more tousled than usual. There was a broad grin on his face. Evidently the night and the music had been satisfactory

'Did you hear me?' he asked.

'It would be difficult not to!' I exclaimed, adding that I had not known that he was so versatile.

He smirked. 'There's a jolly good echo down there! When I bark it goes round and round and *round*. It's lovely!' I said that I was glad he found his accommodation to his liking and that presumably it was quite gratifying having so many old bones at his disposal.

'Well, not specially,' he replied. 'You see they're all sealed up; and in any case even if I could get at 'em I don't suppose there would be much meat hanging around.' I suppressed a shudder and turned the conversation.

15

The Dog's Diary

I was a bit fed up with my master doing a bunk like that and leaving me all alone. But Maurice has been unusually helpful, and this cemetery set-up is pretty good. I like nosing about among the gravestones – you never know what you might find (apart from Maurice of course). At the moment there's a bit of a problem with my grub – haven't had a decent tin of Muncho for some time. Dustbins are all right as far as they go but they don't go far enough. Nothing really beats a human hand dishing out the fodder on a regular basis. Maurice says that now I've found my bearings it's time I started to edge my way into the vicarage itself. The way to do it he says is by subtle stages so as not to startle F.O. Don't quite know what he means by that – after all either you're *there* or you're not! Maurice's mind is a bit tricky and I don't always follow it.

He tells me that once I'm in the house I should be on my *best* behaviour and to keep wagging my tail. Says I should do it with Brio. Who Brio is or where he comes into it I'm not sure but I like wagging my tail and can do it jolly well. He says that now and again I ought to sit up and beg. Apparently humans approve of that. But I told him begging was for sissies and I wasn't going to start on that lark! Still, Bowler used to teach me how to die for my country That's an easy one – you just flop on to the ground and lie doggo until some human pats your head and gives you a biscuit. I might try that instead. After all, if I can settle in the vicarage I shall have a brand new master, a warm home, regular food and this crypt to bound about in. It's nice down here with all the old tombs (though a bit cobwebby which makes me sneeze but I don't mind that). Maurice thought I might be lonely in the night but there's plenty to do what with chasing the spiders (they've had a nasty scare I can tell you!) and listening to all those old ghosts gabbling on. If I told Maurice about that he would think I was barking! But you know we dogs have a sort of sixth sense which cats don't understand.

16

The Vicar's Version

Evensong had gone smoothly and was moderately well attended. It was my first service since returning from Sussex and I was gratified to be approached by a number of the congregation enquiring after my holiday and welcoming me back. The prospect of the following Sunday's sermon delivered without threat of Elizabeth's simpering gaze suddenly seemed quite congenial. I was determined to make it a really good one, and so even during supper I was busily polishing the finer points of its text.

After washing up I took the script into the sitting room where Maurice was lounging, poured myself a whisky (blended of course, Rummage having demolished the malt), settled comfortably on the sofa and started to appraise the finished version. I was happily absorbed in this when there was a loud knocking at the front door. (Why is it that policemen always knock and never ring the doorbell even when there's a perfectly good one staring them in the face?) I knew immediately what it was and scuttled into the kitchen to dispose of the whisky. An excessive reaction perhaps, but you must understand that in such matters impeachable respectability is the essence! The porch light was on and through the glass I could see the blurry outline of two dark shapes. Taking a deep breath and adopting a neighbourly smile I opened the door.

'Good evening, sir,' said the taller. 'I am Detective Inspector March, and this here is Detective Sergeant Samson. Hope you don't mind us calling at this hour but we're making routine enquiries about the death of one of your parishioners, a Mrs Elizabeth Fotherington. We did call some days back but your friend Mr Rummage said you were away, so...'

'Yes, yes,' I beamed, assuming my genial vicarish voice. 'Do come in, officers. You're quite right – I was having a few days at the seaside. It's not often that one gets a chance to enjoy the old briny!' I suppose their reference to Rummage must have brought the latter's phrase to mind and I winced inwardly as I heard myself repeating it. However, it seemed not unsuited to vacuous bonhomie and I ushered them into the sitting room smiling broadly. As I did so it occurred to me that in the circumstances perhaps this was not *quite* the right note to strike and I hastily composed my features into a more sober cast.

The evening was dull with an unseasonable chill in the air and as I feel the cold I had lit a fire. It burned brightly in the grate, and stretched out on the rug lay Maurice, snoring gently. It was a convivial scene and I liked to think created just the right image of cosy domestic innocence. Much of course depended on Maurice continuing to doze. Awake and in truculent spirits he could change the mood in a trice.

I invited them to sit down and waited with a look of co-operative enquiry on my face. They were an oddly matched pair. The senior man, March, was about fifty: thick-set, jowly, and with a slow rumbling voice which reminded me vaguely of one of those shunting railway engines of my childhood. In those days, listening in the night, I had found the sound oddly comforting; that evening it seemed merely tedious. Samson the sergeant looked like an emaciated whippet. He could not have been more than thirty but the pale pinched face and greasy thinning hair gave him an air of broken-down seediness not normally associated with Her Majesty's law enforcers. I wondered vaguely if he could by any chance be a relation of Nicholas Ingaza. Notebook gripped, he perched stiffly on the edge of the chair, his darting eyes taking in everything in the room. I noticed the nicotined fingers and ingratiatingly offered him a cigarette. His face took on an almost human quality as he craned forward to take it, but he was forestalled by a glare from March.

The questioning commenced. As such things go (I assumed) it was fairly straightforward. How long had I known the deceased? Was she a regular churchgoer? Had she ever shown symptoms of worry or stress? Could I think of any reason why someone should wish her dead? What were her relations with the rest of the community? Had she ever discussed anything of an intimate nature with me? (No fear, I thought!) When had I last seen her? 'At church on the Sunday morning,' I replied piously. Thus the questions took their routine course (nothing being said about the will, I noted) and I answered them easily and blandly.

'Well, thank you, sir, I think that's all we need,' rumbled March. He got up to go, but suddenly the whippet spoke.

'Keen bird-watcher are you, sir?' His voice had that thin nasal twang, again slightly reminiscent of Nicholas's. Ornithology was not a topic I had particularly prepared for and I had no idea what he was talking about. Perplexed, I mumbled something about feeding blue-tits.

'It's just that I notice you've got a nice pair of field-glasses up there.' He nodded in the direction of the bookcase where sitting in one of the alcoves were Elizabeth's binoculars. I had shoved them there on my return from Brighton intending to put them away later but promptly forgot.

'Ah, those...' I exclaimed, having no idea how I was going to continue. 'Er – yes ... *racing!*' I announced triumphantly 'Always go when I can – which isn't too often these days I'm afraid. Ha! Ha!' My voice sounded hollow and Samson stared expressionlessly. It was as if he knew, as I certainly did, that I hadn't been near a racecourse for a good twenty years.

However, March seemed to swallow it and said lugubriously, 'Nice to think that the Reverend follows the gee-gees. We all have our hobbies. It's the dahlias with me.' I wondered if it was the dogs with Samson and prayed that neither would ask a tip for the St Leger.

When they had gone I sat for some time replaying the interview in my mind, cursing my carelessness with the binoculars and staring morosely at Maurice who by now had woken up. 'If it's not one thing, it's the bloody other...' I muttered. Maurice seemed to concur for typically he turned his back on me and swished his tail.

A week or two had passed and by now I was well back in the parochial swing of things. The new hassocks had proved a great success, their embroiderers duly applauded and the candlesticks admired. My carefully prepared sermon – 'As We Forgive Them That Trespass' – was equally well received and knocked Rummage's on self-denial and the ordered life into a cocked hat. With Elizabeth out of the way things were rapidly getting back to normal. However, I knew very well that this was a false dawn for there was still the tiresome presence of March and Samson, let alone the so far mythical Violet Pond. She, of course, I was bound to meet, either in my capacity as vicar sympathetic to her mother's untimely demise or as a resented opponent in disputing the will. Judging from Bowler's references, the latter was the more likely. This prospect cast a shadow over the otherwise sunny agenda of my parish duties and I was haunted with lurid pictures of the shortchanged Pond.

However, such images were quickly dispersed by some astonishing news: Reginald Bowler, who had accosted me only a few days previously, had apparently decamped to South America taking a good part of the bank's deposits with him! I was apprised of this bombshell by Miss Dalrymple who telephoned in a state of such manic excitement that at first it was impossible to grasp what was being said. Eventually her words became clear and were indeed later confirmed by reports from other quarters. The local paper was in its element – RESPECTED BANK MANAGER TAKES THE MONEY AND RUNS – and once more Molehill was plunged into a flurry of furtive delight and speculation. Such was the collective shock that it almost eclipsed the 'incident in the woods' but the latter was soon back in the limelight for the two events became swiftly linked in the public's imagination. Bowler the fugitive embezzler was fast becoming Bowler the assassin. While deploring the illogicality of this (and even feeling a grudging sympathy for the maligned), I could not help savouring its convenience.

Like everyone else I was intrigued by the affair. What on earth had possessed the man! Money of course: that was the bald fact, but what about the *truth?* What recalcitrant impulse had prompted that bumptious, dull little man to kick over the traces and embark on such wild drama? Fury, malice, envy? Frustration at being balked of a rich widow? A belief that the world and Mrs Fotherington owed him a living? Or perhaps like the Reverend Digby

Purvis fear of a blank and lonely future? Or was it, after all, just further proof of Bowler's crass stupidity? I was inclined to the last but reflected that whatever the reason it must have taken the hell of a nerve.

While it was comforting to think that this new turn of events might deflect any possible attention from myself, it remained a tense period. There was still the problem of the will (March's silence on that matter being ominous rather than consoling), and I was also nagged by Samson's allusion to Elizabeth's binoculars. I really ought to get rid of them somehow... Something else was bothering me too which at the time I could not put my finger on, but it teased away at the back of my mind and I was worried that I couldn't place it. Fortunately the piano continued a comforting refuge and I returned to it as often as time would permit.

It was on one such occasion when I was practising some Scarlatti that there was a gentle scratching sound at the sitting-room door. Assuming it to be Maurice I told him to shut up, and continued with my playing. After a little I had a distinct feeling of being not alone in the room and turned my head expecting to see the cat meandering about.

148

There was no cat. What *was* there, sitting solidly on its haunches, head tilted on one side, was a dog. At least, that is what I took it to be. There were certainly canine features but judging from the rivulets of matted hair and large splayed paws it could equally have been a miniature Yeti. I stared nonplussed, and then of course recognition dawned. The last time I had seen this creature it had been wearing a pink bonnet and lurching along the pavement like some mournful but oddly decorative Quasimodo. What Bouncer was doing here – for it was he – thumping his tail rhythmically in the middle of my carpet, I had simply no idea.

I continued to stare and he in turn stood up and accelerated the wagging. The bushy metronome began to get on my nerves and sharply I told him to stop. To my surprise he ceased immediately. I say 'surprise' because I had become so inured to Maurice's dumb insolence that to have an animal actually do my bidding was a novelty not without charm. There was a sudden explosive sneeze, and then with tail stilled he started to approach me in a sort of shuffling gait and made one or two attempts to sit up and beg. These were not terribly successful and feeling a trifle sorry for him I gave him a pat on the head. When I withdrew my hand it was covered with cobwebs!

'Now look here, Bouncer,' I protested, 'you can't stay here, and if Maurice sees you there'll be fireworks!' At these stern words he promptly flopped to the floor and seemed to go fast asleep with his head lolling on my right foot. Almost instantly the door was pushed open further and the cat sidled in. He stalked around quite indifferent to the dog's presence and then, without any warning, took a flying leap straight on to my lap. Never before had he made such an overture and I was both shocked and flattered by this attention. Actually it was distinctly uncomfortable not to say excruciating: Maurice has exceptionally sharp claws and to retain his balance on my thin knees he had to use them with some force. However, after a little we were both able to relax and he started to purr – albeit I felt in a slightly menacing way. So there I was, pinioned by Maurice and feet blocked by the now snoring Bouncer... It seemed that together they had requisitioned me.

17

The Vicar's Version

Violet Pond's visit was as tiresome as I had foreseen. It was a Sunday afternoon and I had just returned from a sedate but pleasant luncheon given by one of my parishioners. Coffee had not been served and so I had made myself a cup at home, and was just settling down to enjoy it with the Sunday papers when I heard the gate click. A woman was walking up the path: thirtyish, bulky, and wrapped in a beige gaberdine raincoat with matching drooping hat. Instinctively I knew that it was Violet Pond and glanced quickly at the ankles – yes, the same thick-cut variety. Obviously Fotherington's daughter.

After the initial pleasantries and consumption of the proffered coffee we got down to brass tacks. Or rather she did. It started fairly moderately with her pointing out that her mother had always been vague and her grasp of figures shallow in the extreme: clearly she had confused £25,000 with

£250. Now, although Elizabeth was a feather-brain, to give her her due she had not been a cretin. Even she would surely have distinguished £25,000 from £250. I said as much to Mrs Pond who immediately accused me of presuming a knowledge of her mother's mental capacity that I could not possibly have. I gave a wintry smile and she took another line.

Did I know that her mother had promised her dying husband that on no account would she ever leave any of the family fortune to an outsider (least of all, she might have added, to a parson); and that with one or two minor exceptions she, Violet, had always been intended as the sole legatee? Tut-tutting sympathetically, I murmured that if that were the case it was a pity her father had not put a clause to that effect in his will; the matter of her mother's codicil would not then have arisen. She brushed this aside, saying in righteous tones that surely as a clergyman I was above such technical niceties, and didn't I see the *moral* aspect of the matter? The words 'Hang the morality!' sprang to my lips but I restrained myself. Given the wider situation – Elizabeth's untimely dispatch and my central role in it – such a retort might have been injudicious.

She began to get heated and talked laboriously about the iniquity of lawyers, the intrusiveness of vicars, the foolishness of parents, and the injustice of the world in general. Listening to this you would think she was on the brink of penury! It was a wearisome business; and contemplating the pasty complexion and well-padded thighs I wondered whether the offer of a cream bun might stop or at least divert the flow. I am rather partial to cream buns, and on the few occasions when I have run out of mint humbugs will buy a couple on my way home from the early service. (It's surprising how one craves sweetness at that hour!) I had been looking forward to the one left in the fridge from the previous day but was ready to make the sacrifice if it would calm the Violent Pond.

'I say,' I said genially, 'would you like a cream bun?' She stopped and looked impatient as if about to wave the suggestion aside, but then seemed to think better of it and asked warily where I got them from. Personally I am not one to look gift buns in the mouth and thought this question a trifle churlish. However, I told her the name of the baker and she made grudging acceptance.

I went into the kitchen, relieved by its

silence; put the kettle on, got out a plate and knife and hunted for a napkin. Maurice was on the window-sill gazing intently at the sparrows on the lawn. Absent-mindedly I tweaked his tail. It was fortunate he was so engrossed otherwise there might have been a minor fracas. As it was, he continued his drooling vigilance oblivious of my presence. Just as the kettle boiled, heavy feet sounded in the hall and I realized she was coming into the kitchen.

'And what's more...' she began. And then stopped abruptly, staring past me at the window-sill. 'My God! There's that foul cat of Mother's! What's it doing here?'

'Are you sure?' I said, feigning surprise.

'Of course I'm sure,' she snapped. 'I would know that creature anywhere. It's got a very nasty character. Disappeared quite suddenly – I hoped it had been run over. What on earth are *you* doing with it?' This was said in accusing tones as if to imply that obviously my greed knew no bounds: not content with getting my hands on her mother's money, I had now apparently purloined her cat. I laughed weakly, saying that I had no idea that the cat had belonged to her mother and it had just turned up one day out of the blue. (That part at least was true.)

'Well,' she said, regarding Maurice with distaste, 'good riddance I say. He's the last thing I want to see again!' And with that she collected her tea and bun and marched back into the sitting room. Before following I glanced at Maurice who, rudely interrupted in his bird-watching, was now crouched on the floor with fur on end and a look of squinting malevolence on his face. I understood his feelings.

Resuming my chair I saw that my mollifying efforts had been of little avail. The sop to Cerberus was all but demolished (leaving a large blob of cream on her lapel), and judging from the knit brows and drumming fingers she was clearly poised for further dispute. I braced myself.

During the few seconds that it took for her to remarshal forces I was suddenly struck by the fact that so far there had been no word of regret regarding her mother's death, nor indeed any reference to its manner. I was grateful for this but found the omission faintly curious. Clearly it was the financial angle that was of primary concern. Some people's priorities were so skew-whiff, I thought primly...

She started to talk again. Retaining an air of polite interest I cast a furtive glance out of the window seeking distraction. Someone was passing the front gate. It was Savage, the blind piano tuner. In an instant I had leapt up and exclaimed, 'Oh my goodness, I quite forgot... It's the piano tuner! He's coming to check the "old joanna"!'

'On a Sunday?' she asked coldly.

'Yes, yes! He's so busy, you know, only time he can manage it... Please excuse me!' And with those words I rushed from the room and down the garden path.

I caught up with Savage and in my agitation clutched him by the shoulder. He whirled round. 'Christ!' he exclaimed.

'No, no,' I cried. 'It's me, the vicar!'

'God almighty, you gave me a turn!'

I gabbled an apology and then said breathlessly, 'Can you come in and tune my piano?'

'What, *now?* On a Sunday?' he protested.

'Yes, I know it's short notice but I really need you!'

'No you don't,' he said. 'I only did yours four months ago.'

'Ah,' I replied sobering slightly, 'actually it's not the piano as *such*. You see–' and here I paused conspiratorially – 'I've got a rather troublesome visitor ... a lady.'

'Oh yes?' he replied, giving a knowing leer.

'No, not that sort of trouble,' I said hastily. 'It's just that I am really rather busy – sermons, you know – and she's taking up more time than I can spare. I'd really value an interruption.'

'I don't know...' he said doubtfully, '...it's all very well but I haven't got my bits with me.'

'You don't need bits,' I implored. 'Just shunt it around, and–'

'*Shunt it around?*' he echoed indignantly.

'You know, strum a few notes here and there, lift the lid up, poke about inside – that sort of thing.'

He gave me what amounted to a withering look and thrust his wrist under my nose. 'What time is it?' I looked at the watch and told him that it was half-past three. He paused, and then with a slow smile said, 'Well, you're a funny bugger, vicar, but yes – I can spare ten minutes, I suppose.'

I had always got on with Savage. He was not one of my congregation, indeed probably not a churchgoer at all, and perhaps it was this that allowed a certain freedom in our relations less easily achieved in my pastoral contacts. We entered the house and I introduced him to Mrs Pond. She gave him a nod and a cursory glance; and ignoring my false insistence that his presence would in no way encumber our discourse, gathered up her handbag and crammed on her hat. I escorted her to the door where to the background of Savage's tuneless tinkerings she assured me that this would not be the end of the matter and that I could expect to hear from her further.

Savage must have heard the door close for the strumming ceased immediately and in the ensuing silence I sat down heavily on the stairs and lit a cigarette. I could have done with a brandy but at four o'clock in the afternoon I suppose one had to draw the line somewhere. He came out of the sitting room grinning broadly.

'That your young lady then, is it?'

'No,' I answered testily, 'that is not my young lady. She's simply the daughter of the late Mrs Fotherington come to discuss one or two aspects of her mother's affairs. She stayed too long, that's all. It got a bit tiring.'

'Ah well, they all have their ways, don't they? A bit of the old kid glove, that's what's needed.' He uttered this with authority and was clearly au fait with his subject. 'Take my wife for instance – she's expecting me about now and there'll be merry hell when I turn up late. But I'll just push the *Times* crossword in her direction and she'll soon snap out of it.'

From what little I had seen of Mrs Savage she was not one I would normally associate with the *Times* crossword – but of course one can't always tell in these matters. I apologized for keeping him and asked with interest if she ever managed to finish it.

'Oh, *she* just reads out the clues. *I* answer them. Simple really – calms her down and she becomes as quiet as a lamb again.' I was impressed by this and wondered if I should try the device with Violet Pond the next time she came calling. The only problem was I doubted my capacity to supply the answers.

'Well, must be off,' he announced. 'Just time for a few clues before her choir practice. Then when she's out singing her head off I can get at my drum-kit and rev it up a bit.'

'Your *drum*-kit?' I asked in surprise. 'I thought you might be a fellow pianist.'

'Good Lord no! Can't stand the things. It's always been drums with me, even as a nipper.' He paused and then added ruefully, 'Of course, *she*'s not keen ... but then you can't complain. Like I was saying, they all have their ways, don't they?'

'Yes,' I said slowly. 'Yes ... I suppose they do.'

18

The Dog's Diary

I've got used to being here now and quite like it. I miss my nightly walks with Bowler but the graveyard is good fun and F.O. lets me do more or less what I want. Things were much stricter with my other master. Maurice can be a bit trying of course but I'm learning to handle him. I was able to bring most of my treasures with me – my rubber ring, my bit of brown hairy blanket, the lead that I used to chew on when I was a puppy, and of course my special bone collection (which I keep in a very secret place!). At first I put the other things under the sacking in my basket and only took them out at night as I thought the vicar might notice and smell a rat. But I needn't have bothered. He lives in a world of his own, and as long as he's got his fags and his booze and can play that nice piano there's not much that he sees. When I left Bowler's house I couldn't remember where I had put my ball, but F.O. has given me a brand new one. It's got bells on and is JOLLY GOOD; but Maurice complains of course. He has a thing about bells. Bells and bones – they drive him mad!

Still, he did help me lug most of my stuff here when I moved in – although I had to keep dark about the bones otherwise the balloon would have burst all right! Had to wait till he was off mousing and then carry them in secretly. It took a long time and meant going back the next day as well, but I got them all here in the end. At first I put them in the crypt where Maurice had suggested I slept for the time being. One of his better ideas. As a matter of fact I've left a couple of spares in one of its corners just for emergencies but the best are ELSEWHERE.

I can do my baying in private in this place without anyone interrupting or ticking me off. It's got a lovely echo. Don't use it so much now because F.O. is used to me being around and the basket he's given me in the kitchen is really comfy. But I still like to come down here, especially if it's hot or when I need to do some thinking and work things out a bit. It's got a very nice atmosphere.

Mind you, the vicar's a bit rum. Don't know if they're all like that or whether it's just F.O. Anyway I'm not complaining – he's very nice and so forth – but there's something not quite right there. If I say anything to Maurice he'll probably disagree like he usually does. But I feel it in my bones – and I do know a thing or two about bones. You can generally rely on them. Still, I'm not a dog to make trouble, unless I get bored of course, and there's not much chance of that. There's heaps to do in the graveyard. Besides, I've made a new friend: O'Shaughnessy. He's an Irish set-something. Bigger than me – though not as huge as that rotten William who cut me out on Flirty-Gerty. O'Shaughnessy is really funny and mad and you never know what he's going to do next. He's new to the neighbourhood and has come from over the western seas and tells the most wonderful stories and jokes. (Though he talks a bit fast so I don't always get the punch-lines.) I think we are going to get on really well. Not that I don't get on with Maurice, but of course he's a cat (and so has a *very* odd way of looking at the world) and one needs to tread a bit carefully which can get confusing, especially if his tail happens to be in the way. Still, as things go, *so far so blooming good* – as my old master Bowler used to say.

19

The Cat's Memoir

'I think he did it,' Bouncer suddenly announced.

'Who did what?' I enquired.

'Him, F.O. – I think he bumped her off.'

'That's absurd,' I said. 'Can't think where you get such notions. You've obviously been spending too much time in the crypt.'

He looked down at the ground and after a bit said thoughtfully, 'You know, if anyone finds out, he will be debagged and sent to prison, and then what will become of us?'

I explained patiently that he would not be debagged but unfrocked.

'Well, it's all the same,' he muttered.

'No,' I answered. 'It is not all the same. Debagged means to have trousers removed. Unfrocked is to lose one's dress. It is an entirely different process.'

He stared at me blankly for a moment, and then suddenly bellowed: 'Maurice, you are such a PEDAL!'

I was startled by this show of ferocity and recoiled hastily. In the circumstances it seemed injudicious to risk further semantic correction and I withdrew to the lower branches of a tree. Here I remained with eyes tightly closed until the frenzy beneath abated, and then watched as he stalked off stiff-legged in the direction of the crypt.

During the night I reflected upon his extraordinary allegation regarding the vicar. It all seemed very far-fetched and was surely yet another of his muddled vagaries. If, however, by some remote chance he was right and F.O. *had* done the deed, then certainly our position was distinctly precarious. Losing the vicar would mean further upheaval. There had been too much of that recently and I really couldn't face any more, especially as things were becoming moderately comfortable. My favourite tombstone with its sentinel position on the bank overhanging the road was a fair substitute for the gatepost at the end of Fotherington's drive, and I was loath to relinquish it – or indeed the fairly acceptable meals that F.O. was beginning to provide. I would have to speak further with Bouncer and see whether he really did know anything.

The next morning dawned dry and warm, and emboldened by the sunshine I went to the top of the crypt steps and mewed winsomely. Bouncer emerged from the depths in his usual dishevelled state but looking quite genial, clearly having regained his composure after the previous day's tantrum. A night among the bones must have done something to soothe that peculiar canine psyche. Nevertheless, to be on the safe side I made certain gracious overtures, even taking pains to twirl my tail in a way that amuses him.

He seemed receptive. So picking my words carefully I enquired what made him think that the vicar had relieved Elizabeth Fotherington of her tiresome life. He snuffled the ground and pondered, and then said slowly, 'Well, I've been thinking about this for some time actually, but it takes me a while to get things straight so I haven't bothered to mention it before.' I asked how long he had been trying to get things straight, and he said from about a day after the discovery of the body.

That startled me. Not only was I surprised that Bouncer could be so reticent for so long, but I was also piqued to think that he had chosen to conceal his suspicions from me. An acid comment sprang to my lips but in the interests of peace and curiosity I fought it down. Instead I purred softly and said, 'Perhaps by now you have established a case, have some tangible evidence on which to base these allegations?'

'Not really,' he said, 'I've eaten it.' He then started to scratch vigorously and perform other disgusting ablutions. Patiently I waited for this to take its inelegant course. And then deeming the moment right, I asked gently if he could elucidate further.

'Well, you know those mint humbugs he's always munching – Jumbo Johnnies – the ones he eats when he's not puffing a fag?' I nodded in vague recall. 'When I found the corpse there was half a packet of them spilled all over her feet.' He looked at me expectantly as if awaiting some awestruck gasp.

Naturally none was forthcoming and with waning patience I said dismissively, 'My dear Bouncer, mint humbugs are two a penny. Anyone might have dropped them.'

'Mint humbugs may be two a penny: Jumbo Johnnies are two for threepence. They are a rare quality brand and cannot be got here in Molehill, not even in Guildford. They come–' he added dramatically – 'from the most special place in the world: HARRODS!'

He aspirated the name with a reverential flourish, as if that obviously clinched the case. (How he had obtained such insight into confectionary matters I do not know. Possibly living with Bowler had something to do with it. Knowledge of comestibles – their marketing and retail distribution – might I suppose feature in a bank manager's grasp of commodity values; but in any case it was the sort of trivial piece of nonsense which could well have occupied Bowler.) 'Yes,' I conceded, 'that does narrow it somewhat. But the link remains tenuous, to say the least. You will have to do better than that, old boy.'

I could not resist injecting a note of patronage into my words, but this was lost on Bouncer who went on doggedly: 'Jumbo Johnnies Special Humbugs were found at Fotherington's feet. F.O. likes Jumbo Johnnies, always has a few on him. These can only be bought from Harrods. Every other month F.O. goes to London for one of those Church meetings in the Brompton Road. When he's there he stocks up with the humbugs and so has a constant supply.'

'Yes, yes,' I retorted impatiently. 'Has it occurred to you, Sherlock, that there might just be another person in the area who has a penchant for Jumbo Johnnies, goes regularly to Knightsbridge and wanted Fotherington dead? Indeed,' I continued scornfully, 'how do you know that she didn't have an insane nephew who was manager of Harrods' sweet department and, sick of the tiresome old aunt and impatient for her money, sneaked down to Molehill in the dead of night – pockets *of course* stuffed with Jumbos – did her in, and then returned to London to dispense gob-stoppers to crazy clerics!' On these last words my normally modulated tones had risen to an unseemly screech. Catching my breath I stopped abruptly, annoyed by my loss of aplomb.

Bouncer seemed quite unperturbed, and in the ensuing silence said quietly, 'Yes, but why should the nephew drop a gold cigarette lighter with the initials F.O. on it? Unless, I suppose, his name was Fred Ogle.'

'Why indeed...?' I started to hiss. And then stopped, hardly able to register what had just been said. I fear my astonishment showed itself only too plainly, for Bouncer exclaimed in chummy tones, 'I say, Maurice, close your mouth or you'll swallow a fly!' This *witticism* was accompanied by the usual explosions of shouts and snorts integral to his puerile humour. There followed a brisk bout of leg-cocking by which time I had recovered my wits and could speak firmly to him.

'Bouncer, what lighter are you talking about?'

'You know – the one F.O. always used to carry and which Bowler was so jealous of. The one he said made F.O. look like a smarmy pansy... Maurice, what *is* a pansy?'

'For goodness sake!' I expostulated. 'This is no time to be discussing horticultural matters. Tell me what you did with the lighter! Did you eat it?'

He stared indignantly. 'What *are* you talking about? Of course I didn't eat it – haven't got elephants' teeth, you know.' I considered the sarcasm uncalled for and reminded him icily that I had distinctly heard him say earlier that he had consumed the evidence.

'Oh, that was the humbugs,' he said carelessly. 'I *buried* the lighter.'

I swished my tail and took a deep breath. 'So you buried the lighter as you do your bones?'

He nodded.

'When exactly did all this eating and burying take place?'

'About two minutes after I found the body.'

'You never mentioned that when you were telling me what happened,' I said accus-

ingly. 'Innumerable allusions to those confounded rabbits but not a word about the
really crucial thing!'

'Oh well,' he said vaguely, 'you know how
it is...'

'No, I don't actually. I don't know at all! I
consider your secrecy the height of–' It was
pointless pursuing it. He had moved off and
was sniffing ferociously around the trunk of a
tree lost in his own world of earth and smells.

It was galling to think that for all this time
Bouncer had been sitting on such vital
information without even hinting that he
knew something that I didn't. It was vex-
atious in the extreme. It was also puzzling for
I could not decide whether Bouncer was
beginning to show signs of that low cunning
possessed by many of his tribe, or whether it
was yet further proof of his general empty-
headedness. Either way, I felt a sulk coming
upon me and repaired beneath a holly bush.

20

The Vicar's Version

The scandal of Bowler continued to tantalize respectable Molehill and the press milked his putative link with Elizabeth's death for all it was worth. In fact it was worth very little. Lack of reported evidence plus police denials persuaded public interest that this was a blind alley in which it no longer wished to play. Other areas of speculation were sought and rumours abounded: the fugitive was an international con man wanted by Interpol, he was living in luxury running a string of whores and racehorses in Montevideo, he was a Russian spymaster, a dope peddler, his uncle was Fatty Arbuckle... Thus Molehill happily indulged the more lurid flights of its busy imagination while I got on quietly with my daily rounds. And then inevitably what I had feared made its appearance in the local rag:

MURDER VICTIM'S LEGACY: VICAR RICHLY REWARDED

A little bird tells us that the Rev. Francis Oughterrard, special friend of the late lamented Elizabeth Fotherington, has been generously remembered in her will. Although a comparative newcomer to the parish, the Reverend had clearly made his mark with Mrs Fotherington; and while we commiserate with his personal loss we rejoice in his well-deserved windfall. It is, alas, a mark of our times that churchmen and other spiritual leaders receive scant recognition of their worthy endeavours, and the *Molehill Clarion* applauds the lady's generosity and wishes the vicar well in his good fortune.

The unctuous tone and coy innuendo sickened me (as did the careless misspelling of my name), but I doubted whether the intention was to stir suspicion regarding the crime itself. More likely it was just the press's usual fascinated absorption in the private lives of clergymen and scoutmasters. Though there was also surely that sly hint of some predatory intent on my part which might prove dangerous. It was publicity I could well do without and I spent worrying hours trying to decide a line of action. Quite apart from the main problem it was in any event a disgraceful infringement of privacy, and I thought that the allusion to a special friendship might even border on the actionable.

Finally, however, working on the principle that the less said the better I decided to do nothing. Given the special nature of my circumstances I felt that to swallow pride was a more prudent course than getting embroiled in dispute with the Fourth Estate. The article was short and on an inside page, and even if raising a few prurient eyebrows it would with luck be of only passing interest. Thus having persuaded myself that all would be well I returned to the reassuring boredom of the Confirmation lists, and then to bed.

My complacent hopes were ill founded, for the next day the paper published a follow-up article. Clearly Violet Pond had been at work:

ANGUISHED DAUGHTER SPEAKS OUT
Vicar's Right To Money Questioned
Mrs Violet Pond, grieving only child of murder victim Elizabeth Fotherington, has questioned the validity of her mother's substantial bequest to the Rev. Francis Oughterard.

'There has been a dreadful mistake,' she tearfully told the Clarion's reporters last night. 'My mother was a naive lady with little head for finance and easily influenced by emotional pressures and passing whims. This had always worried my dear father who must be turning in his grave to know that his hard-earned capital which he *passionately* wanted to remain in the bosom of the *family* is to be so wrongly diluted...!' At this point Mrs Pond broke down but rallied valiantly and smiling through her tears emphasized that in no way did she blame the Church, nor of course her mother – 'lost in a maze of matters she did not understand' – but there had been a terrible travesty of moral justice, which coming on top of everything else was simply too hard to bear. She was sure that the Church would understand and take the appropriate action.

Hell's teeth! I thought, savagely hurling the newspaper at the cat. It was less the threat to the legacy that worried me than the disturbing attention it created. Confound the woman, she was as bad as her mother! Worse really, for she had an intelligence, a low cunning quite lacking in the latter's idiocy. Fate – or the ghost of Elizabeth – was forcing my hand and I should have to act after all.

One thing was certain: I had no intention of meekly handing over the funds to the 'bosom of the family' – i.e. Violet Pond! Nevertheless, they would have to be got rid of, that much was obvious. Above all it was imperative that I appeared without a hint of motive.

At the time when it happened I had of course a very definite motive: the suppression of noise and maintenance of peace. Well, that move had backfired all right! I brooded for a while on the Macbethean ironies of the situation, even seeing myself as tragic hero caught in a proliferating web of self-made doom and raw coincidence. The reverie was interrupted by Bouncer who, taking advantage of Maurice's hasty exit, had brought in one of his bones which he was now busily gnawing with gagging relish. The throaty sounds returned me to the pressures of the moment and I started to ponder on to whom I could offload my 'well-deserved windfall'.

At first I thought some ecclesiastical cause would fit the bill – a modest endowment for a theological scholarship, much-needed donations to the Diocesan Repair Fund, support for indigent clergy perhaps... No, none of these. Such a transfer might pander to the view of the Church as a self-serving club and thus play straight into the hands of the martyred Pond. Instead, just for a fleeting second an image of the charitable Mr Gladstone and his fallen women came to mind; but as a focus for philanthropy the latter would hardly enhance my position. I could envisage the headlines only too well: TARTS TO RECEIVE VICAR'S HUSH MONEY. BISHOP DENIES ALL...! Eccentric gestures had their place, I mused, but in this case securing a broad public sympathy was vital and it was unlikely that Molehill was ready to endorse charabanc holidays for ladies of the night.

I racked my brain trying to work out what worthy causes evoked most popular sentiment and over which I could not be accused of personal or professional bias. The young? The old? Dumb animals? Yes, all three were in the front frame and I could do a lot worse than share the money amongst them. These would surely fit the bill and presumably do a bit of good along the way as well. However, having decided *what* there was also the question of *where*. To make donations to large national organizations would certainly be well regarded, but to ensure personal gratitude and loyalty – and thus further defuse suspicion – it might be more practical to target local needs.

My mind roved over the area's possibilities and finally alighted on the ramshackle barn which served as a venue for the Cubs and Brownies. *That* would be appreciated, I thought: a brand new community hall where Badgers and Pixies could cavort, tie knots and sing peculiar songs to their hearts' content! Already I could see the beam of approbation on the faces of their parents and grandparents. And thinking of the latter – what about setting up a special Pensioners' Christmas Party Fund? Properly invested, the money could generate gallons of beer and acres of bangers in perpetuity – far more fun and sustaining than the current dreary fare of weak tea and hard mince pies. And instead of the usual mix of bars of soap and plastic combs we could supply *real* presents: tins of ham, half bottles of whisky, curling tongs, and inexhaustible sets of garden gnomes... Why, we might even afford a professional cabaret artiste who would surely be much more entertaining than Mavis Briggs and her interminable recitations.

The idea took quite a grip on me and I must have been showing signs of excitement for I noticed that Bouncer had ceased his gnawing and was casting me furtive looks from under his fringe. Catching his eye I was reminded of my third needy category: animals. I paused here, feeling that in harbouring him and the awful Maurice I had perhaps already done enough for our dumb friends; however, if there was anything left over presumably a few hundred to the Dogs' Home wouldn't go amiss.

I leaned back in the chair mulling over these ideas, when all of a sudden came the flash of sheer genius – the Elizabeth Fotherington Memorial Prize! An annual prize to be awarded to the chorister who in the judgement of the choirmaster, vicar *and* congregation (a whiff of democracy always impresses) had contributed most to the musical life of the parish and its choir. That little stone would surely settle a few birds! There could be a special award ceremony with plenty of pomp and processing and much mentioning of Elizabeth's name. I even wondered whether one might go so far as to commission an anthem to mark the occasion, to be sung by the whole congregation and led by the chosen chorister. I could hear myself proclaiming it from the pulpit – 'We are now going to sing the Elizabeth Fotherington Anthem. All please stand!'

I rather liked the sound of that and

rehearsed it out loud a couple of times, something that seemed to distract Bouncer even further. He had now completely jettisoned his bone and was standing staring at me with that intent baffled expression that he often adopts and which can be quite unnerving. It had the effect of bringing me down from the wilder heights of fantasy but not before I had exclaimed jubilantly, 'Trounced, Mrs Pond. Trounced!' (My recall is not exact and I think the original phrase had something to do with legacies and fundaments.)

Still chuckling, I went into the study to find my cigarettes but as I was crossing the hall the telephone rang. It was Clinker. What he had to say soon took the smile off my face, and once more I was engulfed in a pall of foreboding...

The bishop's news was as bleak as it was shocking. In bland, avuncular tones he had proceeded to tell me that while he was perfectly satisfied with my running of St Botolph's he felt that 'by and large' and 'on the whole' my special talents(!) could be better employed in a different setting, namely as chaplain to the superannuated residents of St Chad's Rest Home for Church of England

Clergy. This was thirty miles from here in the middle of what I can only describe as a semi-industrial wasteland. I had once had occasion to visit the place and it had not been an enlivening experience; for days afterwards I had been haunted by that doleful line of Betjeman's, '...old and ill and terrified and tight'. Old of course the residents certainly were; but in various degrees so did the other adjectives apply and the prospect of a permanent transfer appalled me. Rummage had once jovially referred to it as the Home for The Clapped-Out. Was this now to become *my* home, and how soon would it be before I too reached that condition – or was I perhaps more than halfway there already?

These were grim thoughts but the knife was given a further twist by Clinker's airy announcement that he was thinking of replacing me with Rummage. Why Rummage, for God's sake! According to Clinker he had acquitted himself remarkably well in my absence, had exerted such a *stirring* influence on the parish. (That was true, I thought: he had given them such a kick up the backside that they were still reeling from the shock and had welcomed my return with near grovelling relief!) What Molehill needed, the bishop opined, was someone of

Rummage's dynamic calibre to drag it into the twentieth century and deliver a spiritual depth-charge – whereas I, apparently, was ideally suited to ministering to the mellow and moribund. (He didn't use that word but it was obvious what he meant.) He added benignly that he was also worried about the strain that the Fotherington/Pond business might be putting upon me and that doubtless I would be glad of a chance to 'get away from it all'. Whether I was supposed to thank him for his thoughtful compassion I don't know, but I certainly didn't. He concluded by saying that since he was due here the following week for the Confirmation Service, he would drop in for a private chat the next day so we could 'explore the matter more fully'.

What an end, what a prospect, what a sell-out! To think that I had staked everything, confronted the very jaws of Avernus to preserve my peace and sanity, when all along these were destined to be snatched away by the vagaries of some meddlesome bishop. Fate was really having its field day. What the hell now? Oh, *what* the hell now!

I collapsed into my chair in the study where despite such misery I couldn't help noticing that Bouncer was again staring at me intently. This time, however, he looked thoughtful rather than baffled, and I was surprised and quite moved when he came over, sat at my feet and put his chin on my knee. I ruffled his fur absent-mindedly, and somehow that woolly contact had a steadying effect. I calmed down and slowly began to gather my thoughts and devise some sort of defence against the bishop's move.

Slowly, amid sips of whisky, the seeds of a strategy began to form. I say 'seeds' because nothing very clear was emerging, and what finally did was distinctly crude rather than inspired. I would get him drunk: completely and appallingly legless in Gaza! I thought of Nicholas and his hints about Clinker's riotous past. (What *was* it at Oxford that had made him so soft on Nicholas at the seminary?) I thought of his alleged penchant for cocktails, his inability to resist 'White Ladies', and the disastrous effects they had on his behaviour. Just supposing that when he arrived to 'explore the matter more fully' I could somehow give him a whiff of earlier days, get him so gloriously tight that the ensuing shame would render the very names of Molehill and Oughterard anathema. With such fearful memories he might be only too glad to let sleeping vicars lie... It was a long shot of course, an absurdity. But nothing ventured nothing gained, and – as I had noticed once before – when desperation drives, anything does tend to go.

21

The Cat's Memoir

The binoculars were still there gathering dust on the shelf where he had left them, but their strap had unfurled and was now dangling down in the most tantalizing way. Naturally, I could not resist giving it the merest tweak with a passing paw. They were more precariously balanced than I had supposed, and the instant I pulled they came tumbling down, narrowly missing me by a whisker.

The crash woke Bouncer who leaped up and roared, 'You clumsy oaf! What did you do that for!' Well, as you can imagine, I was not having any of that! Never in my life have I been described as an oaf, let alone a clumsy one, and I certainly wasn't going to tolerate such insults from Bouncer of all creatures. So without further ado I marched over to him, stood on my hind legs, and with both paws delivered a brisk one-two to the snout.

It was a deft little movement and very satisfying. But I had forgotten his propensity for theatricals and from the ensuing scene you would think he had been mauled by a tiger. The noise brought the vicar flapping in, effing and blinding and scattering ash all over the place, but by that time I had withdrawn to the rug where I crouched with eyes tightly shut, snoring vigorously. He picked up the binoculars, collared Bouncer and took both off to the kitchen. There was a noise of a tin-opener at work: presumably the 'victim' being fed a dollop of Muncho. I sat on the window-sill watching the sparrows and saw Bouncer sloping off in the direction of the crypt: obviously down to his lair to lick the imagined wounds. Peace at last and a chance to reflect on the inanity of dogs and parsons.

There wasn't time to reflect for long. A few moments later the back door opened and I observed F.O. making a lolloping bee-line towards the canal which runs behind the hedge in the adjoining field. He had the binoculars slung over one shoulder. I was slightly surprised at this as I had not known him to be a fellow bird-watcher. But you never know with humans, they get sudden and peculiar whims.

Perhaps he was proposing to look at the stars; they seem to do quite a lot of that. Anyway, whatever was going on, he returned half an hour later *without* the binoculars. I must admit to being a little curious. It did not strike me as very logical behaviour but then humans are not given to logic – least of all F.O. Recalling the peevish display after the police visit I assumed his nerves were playing up again. My mind turned to more absorbing matters: the fish in the Veasey lily-pond and how to get at them without suffering further onslaught from those harridans!

The night passed quietly. Bouncer's basket in the kitchen remained empty and he had evidently elected to stay with the murk and spiders in the crypt. I just hoped it had put him in a more accommodating mood. It generally does. I have often noticed that a night among the tombs tends to have a calming effect and makes him more amenable to useful advice. It evidently suits his peculiar temperament; sometimes in fact too well as there are occasions when he emerges with the most extraordinary notions.

The next day I took up my usual position near the crypt and awaited his appearance. He eventually scrambled up the steps wearing an expression of furrowed gravity. I sighed. Clearly this was to be one of those times when some gnomic pronouncement could be expected...

'I've got mange.'

'What!'

'Mange, I've got it,' he repeated gloomily.

'Surely not,' I protested. 'Where?'

'Backside.' I walked round and inspected his rump. There was a small pale patch about the size of a half-crown. Extending a front foot I gave it a tentative probe with my claw.

'Get off my mange!' he yelled, and scuttled into the shrubbery. After a pause I followed warily and found him tearing and munching tufts of grass. I pointed out that such measures were quite unnecessary.

'Yes they are,' he asserted, 'I am ill!'

I let it go on for a bit, the chewing and spewing; and then said, 'There's nothing wrong with you, Bouncer – you haven't got a trace of mange.'

'I have!' he growled indignantly.

'No. What you have is a patch of dried paint that has matted and flattened your fur.

It was obviously part of something you rolled in and now it's making you itch.' He asked if I was sure, and I told him that unlike some animals I had no difficulty in distinguishing paint from mange and just hoped that F.O. had the wit not to call in the vet otherwise we should have to endure the horrors of the pink bonnet all over again. There was a silence while he thought about that and I harried a passing butterfly.

The afternoon was a time of great noise: F.O. at one of his piano sessions. I find these rather wearisome, though small matter I suppose in comparison with the trials engendered by my previous owner. However, I do not share Bouncer's peculiar enjoyment of music (though a violin can be tolerable if played in the upper registers). But there is no accounting for tastes, especially tastes such as Bouncer's; and at least it provides a distraction from his rabid pursuit of bones and female Pomeranians. Thus for half an hour or so he had been lying in the hall apparently enraptured by the din emanating from F.O.'s sitting room, until prompted by the usual greed he had repaired to his basket in search of broken biscuits. These he proceeded to eat loudly. Closing my eyes in an effort to blot out the grinding of teeth and crashing of keys

187

I tried to sleep... In vain.

'Begorrah!' he suddenly exclaimed apropos of nothing.

'Be-what?'

'Be-gorr-ah. It's what the Irish say, you know.'

'No, I don't know,' I answered. 'Only on the stage, not in real life. It's a popular myth put about by the English.'

'O'Shaughnessy says it.'

'O'Shaughnessy is a show-off,' I countered tartly. There was a silence followed by the usual bowl-rattling, always a danger sign.

'Yes, but at least he's *fun*,' he growled.

I was somewhat stung by that, having always regarded myself as a very companionable cat. Clearly Bouncer was unable to grasp the subtleties of my playful wit. His mind is not the most finely honed. However, I was disposed to be indulgent; and changing the subject asked him what he thought about the detectives and whether he had revised his views about the vicar's hand in the Fotherington affair.

'Oh, it was his hand all right,' he said slowly, 'and if he's not careful he's going to put his foot in it too. And then we shall all be in the can! That weedy one's got his measure.'

'Perhaps he has,' I conceded, 'but that won't matter much. After all, *you've* got the evidence – or have dealt with it at any rate!' And I flashed him a kindly smile. I don't often do that and was slightly disappointed that it didn't elicit a stronger response. In fact it did not elicit a response at all. Instead he stared into space and then started to chew his paw.

Assuming that to be the end of the conversation I decided to go for an early stalk in the graveyard. Just as I was halfway through the pet-flap he called out: 'You know, Maurice, you should never underestimate the enemy!'

Of course the dog is ever prone to hyperbole, yet somehow those words cast a blight over what had promised to be a very pleasant ramble. My pouncing tactics quickly palled and I returned to the house in a mood of irritable disquiet.

22

The Vicar's Version

Rather to my surprise the Confirmation Service was a howling success. Clinker, clad in his episcopal raiment, looked almost impressive and preached a very tolerable sermon. The confirmees were appropriately meek and decorous, the choir efficient, and parents duly appreciative both of it and of the mammoth tea provided afterwards by the Young Wives. Even I had a look in, being congratulated on the choice of hymns and the alacrity of the candidates' catechism responses. Indeed, so pleased was Clinker with his own performance and the general smooth running of the ceremony that for one foolish moment I wondered if he might be having second thoughts about my transfer.

Naturally, such hopes were idle. As he took his leave he drew me to one side and reminded me in tones of booming benignity that he looked forward to calling at the vicarage the next day to discuss 'the logistics' of my removal to St Chad's. Luncheon was not required though apparently a light snack would not go amiss. Smiling gamely I gritted my teeth and turned my mind to the finer details of my plan. It was almost five o'clock but there would just be time to nip down to the off-licence to buy some extra gin for the White Ladies and of course the essential bottle of Cointreau. The latter I knew would be prohibitively expensive – but if my ruse worked the cost would seem a bagatelle!

During the evening I tidied the sitting room, made and wrapped some meat-paste sandwiches for the prescribed snack, and worked out the amount and exact proportions of gin, lemon juice and Cointreau that would be needed to blast the bishop to kingdom come. After that I sat down at the piano and made a remorseless attack upon Chopin's Revolutionary Study.

The next morning I was up at dawn: restlessly on edge but feeling a distinct tingle of excitement as I mixed the drinks and rehearsed my part for the coming challenge.

The challenge arrived at midday. From the bedroom window I saw the Daimler draw up smoothly at the front gate. It was driven by Barnes wearing his usual undertaker's expression. Clinker alighted and after addressing a few words to the chauffeur dismissed the car and started up the path. His footsteps must have startled Bouncer who set up a yelping din unsuited to a bishop's reception. I hastily shoved him out of the back door and told him to buzz off to the graveyard. He trotted away happily, and composing my features into a beaming smile I went to the front door and ushered in my visitor.

Clinker looked moderately benign, presumably having partaken of a good dinner the night before and enjoying his time away from the ghastly Gladys. We sat for a little discussing the weather and the Confirmation, and then I suggested that since it was well past midday perhaps he would prefer a small aperitif rather than a coffee. He declined at first, saying that he rarely touched anything at lunchtime, but then weakened. He had no further plans for that afternoon so perhaps after all the merest soupçon of sherry or something mild would do no harm...

I went to fetch the jug and glasses. On my return he immediately launched into the purpose of his visit: Rummage's advent and my departure. When he had originally broached the subject on the telephone there had seemed some small margin for discussion. Not any longer there wasn't. To his mind the whole thing was obviously a fait accompli and he talked enthusiastically about Rummage's innovative energies and my 'natural empathy with the tired and frail'.

From the very start the prospect had appalled me but now the full horror descended as he expatiated upon the domestic advantages of such a move: there would no longer be a vicarage to maintain, instead a small flat was to be provided within the Home itself – 'cosy, compact and right over the shop, as one might say. What could be more convenient, my dear chap!' I could think of few things more disagreeable; and as he went on to outline further loathsome benefits – meals taken with the residents, Scrabble drives, weekly recitals of harp and recorder – I became increasingly morose. Grasping the jug grimly I poured a hefty slug into his glass. If nothing else it might at least check that dismal paean. In fact so intent was Clinker on selling me the assets of St Chad's that at first he did not seem to register what he was drinking. But at the third sip he suddenly stopped talking, gazed at his glass in wonder and exclaimed, 'I say, Oughterard, what *have* you given me?'

'Oh – just lemon juice, drop of gin and a

dash of orange stuff,' I replied carelessly.

'I should think you have!' he chuckled. 'What you've given me is a White Lady – and at lunchtime too!'

'Really, sir?' I said vaguely. 'Is that what it's called?'

'Yes, yes, of course it is. Don't you know that...! Now, as I was saying–' And he took another sip (getting on for a gulp really) and returned to the delights of St Chad's on which he continued to expound while I smoothly topped up his glass.

Well into his stride and clearly enjoying himself, he raised the inevitable subject of Rummage on whose alleged virtues he gave graphic tongue. At last, moving into his peroration and pausing only for another gulp, he finally concluded with the question, 'Wouldn't you agree, Oughterard?'

'Absolutely!' I exclaimed. 'And what's more he's *so* nippy with the censer! In the old days when we were both deacons I tried to imitate his wrist action but could never quite manage it... Such skill, such artistry – those masterly tilts and swoops, the subtle feints and sallies, the exquisite finger flicks, the smooth control. Why, Rummage's sleight-of-hand was legendary! Of course, he's still got that slickness,' I enthused, 'it's just that there's generally less call for him to use it these days, not with the censer at any rate...'

Clinker looked at me blankly for a couple of moments and then said, 'Hm. Ye-es. Well, I daresay you're right, though I don't think I've ever seen that particular display.'

Noting the burgeoning discomfort as he struggled to decide whether he was dealing with a defective or just conceivably being made the butt of some obscure jest, I hastily turned to the subject of his Confirmation address – The Perils of Piety – and congratulated him on its shrewd perceptions. As a matter of fact the sermon had been an interesting one, though I suspect rather wasted on the candidates. We discussed it briefly and I was reminded of Nicholas Ingaza's remark that once upon a time Clinker had been quite bright. However, not bright enough to resist another White Lady; and I picked up the jug for the third time and offered to replenish his glass.

He accepted without demur, nodded appreciatively and settled back expansively in his chair. I asked politely after his family and Mrs Clinker.

'Oh, she's all right,' he said airily, taking another sip. And then added, 'No, as a matter of fact, Oughterard, that's not entirely true. In fact–' and he leaned forward conspiratorially – 'between you and me and...' Here he paused dramatically, and then with slow and careful emphasis added, *'the gatepost* ... she's being a pain in the arse.'

I was a trifle startled by this and made what was presumably the required response, saying in shocked tones, 'Really? Oh dear! A pain in the arse, you say?'

'Got it in one, Oughterard. In ... the ... arse,' he enunciated with slow relish. I cleared my throat, searching for some appropriate comment.

'Well, sir, I'm sure Mrs Clinker must have some uses,' I ventured encouragingly.

'Oh *yes,*' he said. 'She makes a good junket and stewed mince, and keeps the Mothers' Unions off my back; but other than that of course – she's pure pain.' This was said in a tone of masochistic satisfaction, and there seemed no answer to make. In the ensuing silence I took a couple more sips myself, and then noting his eye fixed leech-like on the jug passed it over, suggesting he help himself. He did so liberally.

'Ah,' I said in a knowing voice, 'I understand what you mean – marriage can put its constraints on a chap!'

He looked at me sharply and despite the

rapidly slurring speech said with some asperity, 'Since you've never taken the plunge, Oughterard, I don't see how you can possibly understand at all. However,' and his tone mellowed slightly, 'as it happens you are absolutely right. All work and no play...' makes Jack a pompous old fart, I thought. Then laughing sympathetically I lit a cigarette. He started to scowl, evidently not appreciating the perfectly formed smoke rings now circling his head. But he could make no objection for fear of my retrieving the jug from his side of the table.

'Yes,' I said nostalgically, 'life pre-war was a little freer when we were all young and uncommitted,' adding wistfully, 'There was quite a bit of fun around then!' I stared into the far distance as if musing upon the good old days. Clinker nodded vigorously.

'That reminds me,' I exclaimed, 'you will never guess who I ran into the other day – Nicholas Ingaza. Now *there's* a figure from the past!'

He didn't respond immediately but then cleared his throat and said warily, 'Ah, Ingaza. Yes – yes, I know who you mean of course, but can't say I recall much of him. It was all so long ago...' And his voice trailed off evasively.

'Oh, but you must!' I exclaimed jovially. 'He certainly remembers you. In fact he particularly asked me to give you his best wishes. His *best* wishes.'

'Well, that's very civil of him,' said Clinker stiffly.

'He spoke most warmly about you, said you used to be the life and soul of the party, a real wag in fact. No ...' I hesitated as if trying to remember the conversation, '...actually, now I come to think of it the term he used was *wagtail*. That's it: "He was a right wagtail – *of one sort or another* – was Clinker." Those were Ingaza's very words!' I laughed heartily, repeating the description a couple of times and enjoying the look of discomfort appearing on his face. 'Of course,' I continued, 'Nicholas was always one for exaggeration. What a raconteur!' And I laughed again indulgently.

'What do you mean, exaggeration? What has he been telling you?' Clinker cried.

The hint had been dropped; it would be unnecessary and clumsy to pursue it further. So to reassure him I said quickly, 'Oh, nothing of any account – you know Nicholas. What an idiot! Always was. Funny him popping up like that after all those years but I doubt if one will see him again. Didn't look too well, I thought. No, I should think he's gone for good. Absurd chap really...'

'Yes,' said Clinker eagerly, 'quite absurd.' He glanced around the room seemingly looking for some distraction to seize upon.

'What do you think of the piano?' I asked helpfully. 'It looks a bit workaday but it's in marvellous condition. I'll give you a demonstration in a minute but how about another of these first? It seems a pity not to finish it off. After all,' I added jocularly, 'it's not often we clergy have a chance to indulge!' I pushed the plate of sandwiches in his direction and went into the kitchen to get clean glasses and the reserve jug from the refrigerator.

When I returned he was standing a little uncertainly at the window munching one of the sandwiches and clutching the curtain tightly. He was humming tunelessly but happily in a rumpty-tum sort of way.

'I say, Oughterard, you certainly know how to mix 'em!' he chortled. 'Haven't had such good White Ladies for I don't know how long. In fact,' he went on roguishly, 'haven't had *any* ladies recently, white or otherwise!' He exploded into a series of hiccuping giggles. I smiled supportively, proffered him another glass and sat down at the piano. 'Roll Out The Barrel' would seem an appropriate beginning and I launched into it with gusto. It was the right choice. Clinker started conducting wildly and bawling a cacophonous accompaniment. But it was when I moved into 'Knees Up Mother Brown' that things really took off.

Clutching the corners of his jacket he started to caper about the room doing a fair imitation of Mrs Brown. The faster I played the more frantic the performance, and the good lady's knees-ups soon turned into a spectacular can-can. For a man of the bishop's girth and age his nimble energy was quite impressive. He pranced and trumpeted merrily while pictures wobbled and drinks and books went flying. Quite obviously he was having the time of his life.

As I pounded the keys I noticed out of the corner of my eye that Bouncer was poised in the doorway looking in on the scene. Presumably bored by his own devices in the graveyard, he had come back to the house seeking diversion. He certainly got it. With a sudden whoop of excitement he hurled himself into the room where he bounded delightedly snapping at the bishop's heels. For half a minute or so man and dog cavorted together until somehow Bouncer must have got entangled in the dancer's flailing legs. A sharp yelp was followed by a stupendous crash. I spun round on the piano stool and saw Clinker sprawled on the floor hooting and heaving in a state of helpless mirth. He floundered about for a bit and then looked up at me, closed his eyes, and with a contented sigh passed out.

I went into the kitchen for a cloth to mop up the spilt drinks. Bouncer was there, by now sitting meekly in his basket. He wore a slightly worried expression and seemed surprised when I stooped down to pat his head and give him the remains of the potted meat sandwiches.

The problem was how to get the bishop off the floor. I don't have great physical strength and knew that I was unlikely to be able to cope with Clinker's bulk on my own. Barnes would be due shortly but I didn't particularly want him to see his employer in that recumbent stupor. As I pondered this I heard a movement outside the window and realized that someone had entered the porch. It was too early for Barnes and I feared it might be one of the choristers come to collect his lost music-case.

It wasn't the chorister: it was Savage. He

was holding a garden fork and a small cardboard box. 'I've brought your fork back,' he said. 'Thanks for the loan. Can't think where mine's got to, confounded thing. Have to get a new one, I suppose.' He put the fork down and thrust the box at me. 'The wife thought you might like these – they're fairy cakes. She's always making them and had a few left over.' He warmed to his subject. 'Actually they're not bad really. They've got thick butter cream made with a sort of raspberry-tasting cochineal, and silver balls, and little–'

'How kind!' I beamed, taking the box and hastily putting it to one side. 'Look, I'd appreciate it if you could spare a minute. There's a bit of a problem which perhaps you can help me with.'

'Another one?' he said warily.

'It's not all that serious,' I answered reassuringly, pulling him in and shutting the door firmly. 'It's just that I've got a chap laid out on the floor in the sitting room.'

'Oh yes?' said Savage. I guided him into the room where Clinker still lay sprawled on the carpet dead to the world.

He stared down unseeingly.

'What's wrong with him?'

'Honkers,' I said.

'Ah...' he muttered; and then as an afterthought added, 'Bit early in the day, isn't it?'

'Well, he got a little carried away – you know how it is sometimes.'

'It happens,' observed Savage sagely. 'What do you want me to do?'

I suggested that if we each took an armpit we could perhaps drag him into the hall and prop him up on the stairs. 'His car will be here soon and the chauffeur can take over.'

'Chauffeur, eh!' exclaimed Savage impressed. 'Who is he – the Queen of England?'

'Not as such,' I answered, 'though he sometimes thinks he is.'

We bent down and started to take a grip. As Savage fumbled he must have touched Clinker's stiff collar. 'What's he got round his neck?'

'A dog collar.'

'Crikey!' he exclaimed in awed tones. 'He *must* have had a skinful!' I explained patiently that it was of course a clerical dog collar.

'One of your cronies, is he?'

'As a matter of fact,' I replied with dignity, 'he is one of my superiors.' (I thought it unnecessary to define Clinker's exact status.) 'He is not in the habit of imbibing and overdid it a trifle.'

'You don't say,' replied Savage drily.

It took some time to get Clinker on to the stairs and we were both perspiring from our exertions. To say that he looked the worse for wear would be an understatement. A picture of utter dissolution would be nearer the truth. He was still out for the count, and Savage, finding the purple handkerchief in his pocket, had started to fan the banister vigorously. I gently tilted his hand in the direction of Clinker's face. The draught seemed to take effect for he opened his eyes, glared at Savage and in petulant tones said, 'Can't you *ever* close the door, Gladys!' He then promptly returned to his torpor. I thought that a little sprinkled water might help the revival process and went to the kitchen. When I returned Savage seized the glass and muttering something about shock tactics flung its contents over Clinker. Except that it wasn't over Clinker; it was over me.

At that point the bell rang, and brushing the dripping water from my sleeves I went to open the door. Barnes stood there in his full chauffeur's rig: black peaked cap, tunic, shiny boots and gauntlets. He looked like Conrad Veidt minus the monocle, and I resisted the temptation to click my heels. He stared past me, taking in the crumpled effigy on the stairs. I half expected him to say, 'Mein Gott!' Instead, he gave a low whistle and exclaimed, 'Streuth!'

'I am afraid His Lordship is a bit under the weather,' I said.

'I should think he is!' he observed, adding accusingly while eying my sodden shirt, 'He wasn't under the weather when I delivered him here this morning!'

'Well, he is now,' I snapped, not liking his tone. 'And I want you to help me get him to the car.'

Fortunately Barnes was tall and broad-shouldered, and together we were able to haul the bishop to his feet and gradually lever him out of the front door. As we were making our lurching way down the path there was a shout from Savage, left standing in the porch: 'Hey, what do you want me to do with your fairy cakes?' I did not answer, being too preoccupied manoeuvring Clinker's sprawling feet.

At last, hot and panting, we achieved the Daimler door and heaved our burden into the back seat. Here he basked like some beached seal intoning quietly, 'Knees up, knees up...' Then, with a dying fall the voice faded and was replaced with a rumbling, rhythmic snore.

Barnes climbed into the driver's seat and I

expressed my thanks, adding that I was sure he would treat the matter with the appropriate discretion.

'Oh yes, sir,' he replied impassively, 'you can rely on me. And if I may say so, I hope you will be able to find somewhere to put your fairy cakes.' So saying he drove off down the road at what I felt was an unnecessarily brisk speed.

23

The Cat's Memoir

After the imbroglio with the bishop a period of relative calm had settled upon the household. Taking advantage of the lull I was in the sitting room one day quietly resting after having had what Bouncer would call 'a dust-up' with an unduly fractious mouse. As I sat there savouring the privacy, I noticed that the piano stool's sliding seat was partially open. It covers a deep recess for storing music and I assumed that F.O. had been careless in replacing it. Being a little pernickety about such things, I strolled over to see if it could be closed. Balancing on my hind legs I tried to push the seat back into place with my right paw. The wretched thing seemed to have jammed slightly and my exertions nearly made me lose my balance. Clinging to the side of the stool for support I involuntarily peered into its interior. What met my eyes I can barely manage to tell...

Gaping up at me lay an assortment of variously shaped and *disgusting* old bones. Gnarled, yellowing and smelly, they were arranged neatly in two lines of graduated sizes, looking for all the world like a set of mastodon's teeth. For a nightmare instant I froze, riveted; and then, appalled by such horror, shot to the sanctuary of the window-seat where I brooded long and hard on the iniquity of dogs and their brazen beastliness.

Half an hour later there was a clatter of toenails on the hall linoleum and Bouncer wandered in looking his usual vacant self.

'Bouncer,' I hissed from behind the curtain, 'you have contaminated the music stool!' He whirled around with a startled yelp and then relaxed when he saw my head emerging from the folds of the cretonne.

'Oh, it's you!' he said.

'Of course it's me,' I exclaimed. 'Who did you think it was – Madame Butterfly?' He looked a bit blank and so I launched into a particularly eloquent and well-honed harangue. Among other things this involved Bouncer's barbarism, his eating habits, the grisly state of his basket, and above all his general failure to observe the courtesies due to a cat of my taste and breeding. Its delivery was lucid, measured and lengthy, and it cut not one splinter of ice.

He shifted his paws, wagged his tail, and then in bright confidential tones said, 'You see, Maurice, that stool has really made a prime pantry. It's just the job for bone storage: right size, right temperature, easy to get at, and above all, safe! F.O. never bothers to file his music, and nobody would think of looking there except,' he murmured vaguely, watching a flight of swallows as they swooped past the window, '...the occasional cat perhaps.'

24

The Vicar's Version

My hopes that by plying the bishop with drink I could somehow change his mind vanished the instant his car disappeared round the bend. Standing on the pavement in the waning sunlight, I cursed myself for being such a fool. Surely only a mind severely deranged could have devised a scheme of such preposterous inanity! That the mechanics of the scheme had gone like clockwork was neither here nor there: the consequences would be dire.

For the next few days I drifted in a kind of limbo, caught between a state of nervous tension and vague feelings of anticlimax. At first I thought that the wrath of God would descend in a maelstrom of incense and mitres. But there was nothing. Neither sign nor sound emerged from the palace – just a disquieting silence during which I concluded that Clinker was either languishing under a prolonged hangover or busily marshalling the guns of dismissal. To relieve the anxiety I decided to bath the dog.

This was a task I had not performed before but I thought it might serve as a 'challenging therapy'. Challenging it was, therapeutic it certainly wasn't. The problem was not that Bouncer objected to the bathing procedure but that he loved it too well. With hindsight it is obvious that a good deal of water-spaniel had gone into his mongrel genes, and that, living in the vicarage with only the dry dock of a graveyard to play in, his aquatic instincts had been cruelly thwarted.

However, at the time these thoughts had not occurred to me and I expected sullen resistance. Donning an apron and a determined air I filled the bath, tested the temperature and squirted in a tube of Rosy Bubbles. Then I opened the bathroom door and coaxingly started to call his name... A shaggy cannonball blasted its way past me and with a mighty bound launched itself upon the pink and fragrant waters. The displacement of liquid was huge and explosive: waves drenched the walls, tidal pools undulated across the linoleum, towels festooned themselves with strands of fairy foam and the air was torn asunder with shouts of canine gaiety.

Riots are not normally associated with tiny spaces, nor their participants with less than a certain number. Bouncer, however, had contrived to turn himself into a mob and the bathroom into a waterlogged Field of Mars. Yelping and lunging, he waded around in jubilant glee, chasing the bubbles, worrying the flannel, wringing the neck of the hapless sponge. I did what I could to calm him, even trying a few tentative strokes with the soap, but these gestures only added to his fun. The riot intensified and the waters rose...

The grand finale came when, with tail flailing like a dripping whirligig, he leaped from the bath and laid the mangled remnants of the sponge at my feet. He was clearly proud of his retrieving skills and it seemed churlish to point out that the object was to present the quarry unscathed. Drying him off was a further challenge, and when amidst my struggles I caught the shrilling of the telephone I felt as a flagging wrestler must on hearing the friendly clang of the closing bell. Draping him in a towel I closed the door firmly, went downstairs and lifted the receiver.

As a distraction from my current anxieties Bouncer's ablutions had been a great success. Indeed, so effective were they that the desiccated tones of Clinker's secretary came as a rude shock. He announced stiffly that His Lordship wished to speak to me in an hour's time and this being the case would I kindly make myself available by the telephone at eleven o'clock sharp.

As directed, shortly before eleven and still jaded by my exertions with Bouncer but fortified by some potato crisps and an early gin, I was hovering by the phone dutifully awaiting the bishop's call. It came precisely as the clock was striking eleven.

At first I could barely hear him – one of those not infrequent occasions when the line was in epileptic mode. Certainly quite a lot was being said, but *what* exactly was impossible to grasp. Trying to decipher Clinker's fractured garglings I absent-mindedly helped myself to the remains of the crisps – at which point the phone immediately became crystal clear and Clinker's words thundered distinctly: '...and so anyway, as I pointed out, all things being equal I have decided–' He broke off. 'Oughterard, you are not eating, are you?'

'Oh no, sir!' I spluttered, swallowing hastily. 'At least, not really, just–'

'Of course you are,' he snapped. 'It's like listening to a dray-horse with its nosebag.

Stop it at once!' The imperious directive confirmed my fears that nothing had changed since his brush with the White Ladies and that he was still hell-bent on removing me and emplacing Rummage. Maurice was sitting on the window-sill and I pulled him a face of spectacular distortion. It was met with a glacial stare, and suitably chastened I once more lent ear to the bishop.

'The problem with Rummage,' he was saying, 'is that he's too conscientious, too dedicated. There's so much *zeal* there and I don't want it wasted. Not of course that Molehill isn't a worthy cause, you understand, but there are other parishes *crying out* for leadership, inspiration, succour. Rummage is the man for them! Mark my words.' I cannot say that I had ever thought of Rummage as a source of succour, and was about to say as much when I suddenly saw where things might be leading. 'There are certain parishes, Oughterard,' he continued, 'which need not so much inspiration as *nurture*. A safe pair of hands – that's what Molehill needs, and that's what I think it has in you. More or less, at any rate.' He paused, clearing his throat loudly and lengthily.

When he had finished I said tentatively, 'Uhm – so you want me to stay in Molehill, do you, sir?' There was a snort of exasperation from the other end.

'Yes, Oughterard. I thought I had made that perfectly clear at the beginning of our conversation. You obviously didn't hear me; too busy eating, I suppose.' I couldn't recall engaging in any conversation but refrained from saying so. Instead I asked diffidently what his plans were for St Chad's now that I was no longer destined to be its chaplain.

'Oh, I'll cobble something together for them,' he replied impatiently. 'The main thing is that you are to remain undisturbed in Molehill and the whole matter can now be dropped... Do you understand, Oughterard? Are you listening! *The whole matter can be dropped.*'

Wondering vaguely what sort of cobbled incumbent was about to be thrust upon the residents of St Chad's, I replied meekly that of course I understood, adding as an afterthought that I trusted Mrs Clinker was well and that her culinary skills continued to flourish. This pleasantry was met by a long silence, after which there was a click and the line went dead. I raised my glass.

25

The Cat's Memoir

'I've been given a bath,' he announced proudly.

'So I heard,' I answered. 'And let us hope there is a long interval before the next. I don't think my nerves can stand much more.' He looked put out.

'I thought you would be pleased,' he grumbled. 'After all, you are always going on about my cobwebs and my special smell.'

'Yes,' I retorted, 'but it is a matter of costs and benefits, and in this case the cost was prohibitive. Do you realize the echo that bathroom generates? My poor ears were mangled by your din ... and then there was that puddle seeping on to the landing. Needless to say F.O. never bothered to mop it up, and my tail and paws got soaked!'

'Oh well,' he said indifferently, 'I don't suppose that hurt much.'

'It most certainly did!' I snapped. 'Cats and wet don't mix.'

I was just gearing myself up to launch into a really good diatribe when I was diverted by Bouncer's manner. He had cocked his head on one side, as he does when concentrating hard, and was looking at me with furrowed brows while at the same time slowly wagging his tail. This was accompanied by a rhythmic opening and shutting of his jaws, almost as if he were rehearsing or mimicking something though no discernible sound emerged. The effect was curious and slightly disconcerting.

I was about to resume my polemic, when suddenly in loud but oddly unctuous tones he barked: 'MY DEAR GOOD LADY DO PLEASE BE QUIET!' The words slid out in a rush and hung suspended between us as we stared in mutual wonder. As you may imagine, it was less the injunction to silence that so shocked me as the mode of address on which it was predicated.

Having delivered himself of this extraordinary utterance he lay down and promptly went to sleep. I have to admit to being more than a little rattled; and in the ensuing semi-silence (he rarely sleeps without snoring or snuffling) I brooded deeply, baffled and affronted. Then deciding that it was futile trying to fathom the contortionate workings of Bouncer's mind, and after making a reconnaissance of my nether regions just to be sure, I too curled up and fell asleep.

When I awoke it was to find Bouncer standing over me, peering down intently. When one has been enjoying a peaceful doze it is quite a shock to be confronted with that woolly face thrust so close to one's own. I shut my eyes, hoping that when I looked again it would have disappeared. It remained.

'Ah,' he said, 'about time you surfaced. I've got something very important to tell you.'

'Oh yes?' I replied sceptically.

'Yes. It's to do with F.O. and his lighter.'

'The one you buried?'

'Of course the one I buried – he hasn't got any others, you know!' I resented this and fixed him with a steely eye. He continued. 'You know my friend O'Shaughnessy?' I nodded wearily, expecting a catalogue of the setter's latest exploits. 'Well, he's on good terms with one of the police sniffer dogs and she's told him that there's a move afoot to re-examine the place where the body was found – where *I* found the body.'

'They've already done that,' I said.

'Yes, but not with dogs. Apparently March has copped it from the high-ups for not doing it thoroughly. So they're going to give it another going over. If that lighter's found the vicar will be in for it – and so will we!'

'Well,' I replied, 'the answer is simple enough: you had better run along and dig it up before they get there.'

He looked shifty, and then muttered, 'It's not as easy as that.'

'Why not?' I asked sharply.

'Well, you see, Maurice, sometimes I forget where I've buried things...'

'And this is one of those times, I suppose!'

He nodded.

'But surely,' I protested, 'you must have a rough idea where it is, and I am sure the exact spot will come back to you once you've got going.'

'It might,' he said doubtfully, 'and then again it might not. Doesn't always work like that – and it could take ages!' He seemed so dejected that despite my irritation I felt almost sorry for him.

'Look here, Bouncer,' I said briskly, 'this is one of those rare occasions when your friend O'Shaughnessy might be useful. Go and find him and tell him his services are required. The pair of you must get digging immediately. With his snout and your obstinacy you're bound to unearth it.'

He brightened and began to wag his tail. 'Do you really think so, Maurice!'

'Of course I do. Hurry up! And when you find him report to me. Naturally I shall have to accompany you both to supervise matters.' He raced off and I kept sentinel on the window-sill awaiting their return.

After a short time I saw the two dogs push their way through one of the many holes in the vicarage hedge and went to join them in the garden. O'Shaughnessy was in a state of some excitement, leaping about all over the place and generally indulging in his tiresome acrobatics. It was just as well that F.O. was at one of those tedious bell-ringing exercises otherwise the creature's antics might have attracted even his attention. I told him to calm down and to remember that he was on a privileged and vital mission, and that while I realized sobriety was foreign to his nature he should at least try to cultivate a little discipline. He seemed to accept the admonition quite happily and gave me a broad wink. I don't entirely understand these Hibernians.

Anyway, I marshalled the two of them together and we set off resolutely for the woods.

26

The Vicar's Version

I did not think that they had really done with me, and inevitably March and Samson returned. It was about nine o'clock on a rainy morning when I had just got back from early service to find them lurking in the porch. They were wearing what seemed to be identical fawn raincoats, March bursting out of his and Samson's absurdly large for his weedy frame. They looked damp and melancholy. I let them in, offered coffee which was declined, and once more took them into the sitting room. Here they grilled me. Well, not exactly, but the mood was certainly more abrasive than on the previous visit. To begin with things were moderately all right and I parried their questions with cool assurance. It was only towards the end when the matter of the wretched binoculars was broached that I became really rattled though I liked to think this was not apparent. It was entirely my own fault: I was simply ill prepared.

It had been a great relief disposing of those things in the canal and I had fully intended to have a story all ready to account for their absence should anyone (i.e. *They*) be interested. But what with the distractions of the bishop, the problems of the newspaper publicity, coping with the Violent Pond – not to mention the daily demands of parish duties – the matter of a plausible reason had been temporarily shelved. As things were turning out, not temporarily enough. You must understand that I was in a situation somewhat foreign to my experience and thus not especially practised in these matters.

'We've received an anonymous letter,' began March. 'It indicates you were having a liaison with the deceased. Is that true, sir?'

'Absolutely not!' I exclaimed indignantly and with an inward shudder. 'May I ask where this letter comes from?'

'South America.'

'Oh well, one might have guessed,' I said caustically. 'Hardly anonymous – Mr Bowler, I presume!'

'Yes, sir, that's what we think and we are pursuing its provenance. But in the meantime we rather wonder why the allegation should have been made at all.'

'Obvious, isn't it?' I responded testily,

'Bowler knows he's a suspect and naturally wants to divert attention and involve some perfectly innocent bystander.'

'That's as may be,' he rumbled patiently, 'but what we're wondering is why he should pinpoint *you* – I mean, you being a vicar and all that... After all, there must have been better choices – more plausible, that is.' He coughed. I thought, but could not be sure, that there was a snigger from Samson. 'And of course,' he went on, 'there's the legacy, isn't there? The one that her daughter seems so upset about.'

'Mrs Pond's emotional problems are nothing to do with me,' I replied frostily, 'and besides, the matter of the money has already been taken care of.'

I immediately regretted using that particular expression and wasn't surprised when there was a movement from the whippet's corner and his thin voice snapped out, 'Taken care of, sir? What do you mean by that exactly?'

'What I mean by that *exactly* is that while I was flattered to be mentioned in Mrs Fotherington's will, I decided from the start to pass on the bequest to worthier causes. After all,' I added, easing the tone and chuckling nonchalantly, 'what on earth would a bachelor parson like myself want with that sort of money! There are already various local projects earmarked for the funds – as no doubt you will verify. I am sure Elizabeth would have approved, she was a very charitable lady.'

'Most commendable, sir,' said March, while Samson remained expressionless and, I suspected, unconvinced. 'But there's something else that's bothering me a bit which you may be able to help us with.' I tried to look cooperative and braced myself.

'It's the binoculars,' interrupted Samson. 'On our last visit we noticed you had a pair – which of course isn't unusual – but so did Mrs Fotherington and she probably had them with her at the time she was murdered, bird-watching or some such in the woods.' (You mean *you* noticed, I thought.)

'I am sorry, I don't see the connection. What on earth is the significance of both Mrs Fotherington and myself possessing a pair of field-glasses? Dozens of people have them.'

'Yes, but *are* they yours?'

I was about to answer, 'Of course they're bloody mine!' but just checked myself in time. Instead, in a voice that contrived to sound both patient and pained said, 'I take it, officer, you are insinuating that the glasses I have in my possession belonged to the murdered lady and that for some reason I appropriated them at the scene of the crime – thinking they might fetch a good price, I suppose! Needless to say I am shocked by your suspicions but even more baffled by your reasoning.'

'We're having to check everybody,' said March in a conciliatory tone. 'You see, the problem is that when we searched the house immediately after the discovery of the body, we found an empty binoculars case on the top of her dressing table by the open window. Yet the contents of that case have never been found and it is my idea that she had been using the glasses just prior to going out that morning. She took them with her but, perhaps being in a hurry, didn't bother to take the case. If we could locate them it would be a real help. As it is, it's a bit of a mystery really...' His voice trailed off and he looked pensive and genuinely puzzled.

'But surely,' I laughed in mounting discomfort, 'a discarded case doesn't necessarily mean that she had taken them with her! I mean, perhaps they had been left somewhere else in the house, or one of the staff might have used them and been too frightened to own up. It happens, you know.'

He shook his head. 'Yes, sir, I do know and you can be assured we've pursued all that, naturally. There's no doubt about it, she had them with her all right.'

'I bow to your experience, inspector,' I answered, foolishly allowing a tinge of pique to sharpen my tone.

He ignored it and went on stolidly, 'According to the stamp and style of the case they're quite an expensive and distinctive pair: Zeiss, post-war manufacture. Not uncommon, I grant, but if in the course of our investigations we were to come across such a pair whose case could *not* be accounted for, then naturally we would be quite interested. You get my drift, sir?'

I got his drift only too well. Any moment they were going to demand the items I could not produce and for whose absence I had no explanation. Panic seized me and I cursed my lack of prevision. 'Well,' I said lightly with mouth as dry as dust, 'I suppose you want me to produce mine along with their matching case so that I can be – as I think you would say – eliminated from your enquiries?'

'That's it exactly, sir. If you'd be good enough to fetch yours for us we can check them off our list, and then be on our way to worry somebody else and leave you in peace!' He beamed genially. (Peace! When, when?) I cleared my throat, thinking frenziedly.

'I am sorry, inspector, I can't do that. You see, I have neither my binoculars nor their case, I–'

'Where are they?' barked the whippet.

I fixed him with what I liked to think was a chastening look as various possibilities rampaged through my head: I had taken them to be repaired, they had been stolen, run over by a car, I had lost them on the racecourse, sold them, I had presented them to the winner of the Egg and Spoon Race at my old school – all easily verifiable and/or lame and improbable. 'I was about to say,' I continued with dignity, 'that I have lent them to a friend. He has broken his and wanted some to take on holiday. He'll be back soon, I think, but until then I am afraid–'

'Name?' demanded Samson, pen poised.

Until that moment the dearth of close friends in my life had never really been a cause for concern, but at that point it certainly was; and I was faced with the invidious decision of conferring the privilege of my friendship upon either Savage or Nicholas. Neither of them was close yet one of them was about to be cast in that role. Even in those split seconds I thought wryly of the existential qualities of the choice; but these yielded to a moral imperative. Thus dismissing Savage on account of his wife and his innocent decency, I opted for Nicholas.

'Thank you, vicar,' said March, levering himself out of the chair. 'Don't suppose we shall need to trouble you further. But of course if anything else *should* crop up, or I get any ideas about the deceased's life that you might be able to help me with, we'll be in touch.' I showed them to the door where he turned and said, 'By the way, I've been thinking... I like your idea about the charities – you know, passing on your money like that. A pity more people aren't as generous. Very nice idea, sir!' Judging from his sour expression, I felt that Samson did not share his superior's appreciation (if such it was), but by then I was too exhausted to care.

Beware the ideas of bloody March, I thought grimly, watching them walk down the path and into the road. My immediate impulse once they were safely gone was to collapse on the sofa and escape in sleep. Instead I rushed to my desk and amidst the chaos of papers started to search frantically for Nicholas Ingaza's telephone number.

27

The Vicar's Version

On the few occasions that one really wants to contact someone they are rarely there and one listens with growing gloom to those futile ringings. Thus it was as I repeatedly tried to get Nicholas, all efforts being met with a bleak silence which did nothing for my nerves. It would have been less frustrating had I been able to visualize the instrument's location – see its table, room, or even building. But I had no such picture in mind, no clues as to its owner's habitat. The ringings went on, bleating into blank space. Did Nicholas live in a flat? Or a semi in Kemp Town? A bijou town house on the borders of Hove? A seedy bed-sit above some ramshackle junk shop, its hallway smelling of cabbage and disinfectant? It could have been any or none of these – though my imagination veered, perhaps unjustly, to the last. Nicholas's domestic life was not a subject I chose to dwell on; but I did need his help –

and quickly! Clearly such help was not at hand, and to assuage annoyance I rounded up Bouncer and set off for a brisk walk.

Brisk though the intention, the reality was a fatiguing meander. I do not possess Reginald Bowler's physical resolution nor his commanding tone, so progress was hampered by Bouncer's steely insistence on sniffing at every object and by my fruitless efforts to drag him along. Thus the walk was slow and frustrating and I recalled wonderingly the vision of that dynamic duo when in the days before Bowler's defection they would make their nightly assault upon The Avenue and its purlieus. I pondered whether Bouncer missed Bowler and whether he found his new master small beer in comparison. I hoped not, for in a masochistic way I had grown quite fond of the dog.

Mavis Briggs appeared round the corner and accosted me about some annual poetry reading she was mounting entitled 'Gems of Uplift' – and in which she no doubt would be the principal performer (unless scuppered by the other diva, Edith Hopgarden). She assured me that my predecessor had been a regular patron of the event and had always found it truly inspiring. (Poor Purvis, I thought – so inspiring that he hit the bottle and gave up the ghost.) I showed a bland and evasive interest, and mercifully her ramblings were cut short by Bouncer who at that moment chose to squat down in the road and mount his own event. She passed quickly on.

That over we proceeded at a sprightlier pace; and once back at the vicarage I tried the telephone again and was caught off guard when it was answered immediately. The voice was not Nicholas's and had a strong Cockney accent.

'Er – could I speak to Mr Ingaza if he is in, please?' I asked diffidently.

'You might,' the voice said slowly. 'Who's calling? Not Nigel, is it?' I told him that it was not Nigel but the Reverend Francis Oughterard. I am not sure why I prefaced my name with its clerical title as it is not something that I normally do. Some sort of defence mechanism, I suppose. Anyway, there was a silence and then I heard him yell: 'Nick, Nick ... it's a vicar for you.' Presumably there must have been some distant response as again I heard him shout: 'I don't know ... some geezer who says he's a viCAR.' The term was given its maximum emphasis; and then more quietly down the mouthpiece he said, 'Hang about a bit, he'll be down in a mo.' I hung about, rehearsing my lines and feeling tense.

I could hear the soft footfall, the movement of the receiver, and then those familiar bantering tones. 'Well, there's only one vicar in my life these days – it must be Francis Oughterard. Down in Brighton again? What *will* your masters say!'

'No, actually I'm calling from home. I was just going to–'

'Very wise, Francis! You of all people should never stray too far – don't think you could manage it,' and he chuckled thinly. 'To what do I owe this unexpected but certain pleasure?'

I cleared my throat and asked him if he wouldn't mind doing me a small favour. He said he couldn't imagine what it could be but was always ready to help out an old theology colleague. (Whether such colleagues ever invoked his help I very much doubted. Surely none but a fool would choose to venture into Ingaza's dubious orbit – unless like me they were in dire straits.) I took a deep breath and broached the matter.

'Nicholas, I've been placed in a slightly embarrassing position. You see it's the police, they–' There were sudden peals of laughter from the other end.

'My God, Francis, you haven't! Who'd have thought it – and after all this time! *What* a careless boy...'

He was right in one respect: I *had* been careless, but hardly in the distasteful way he seemed to be suggesting and I resented the imputation. 'No,' I replied sharply, 'it's not that at all, not at all! It's to do with a lady and some binoculars.' This produced more hoots and I cursed my choice of phrase.

'Well,' he said eventually, 'that's not quite my line of country, of course, but having some knowledge of tight corners – as you might say – who knows, I might just be able to help.' There followed another spluttering paroxysm. Had I foreseen the ribaldry my request would provoke I might have thought twice about approaching him. I was distinctly put out and felt his levity uncalled for. He must have sensed my irritation for he simmered down and asked in a tone of seeming concern what the problem was.

Skating carefully around the actual crux of the matter and with the help of some fine pruning I sketched out the peripheral details of the problem, stressing that should the Molehill police contact him regarding his 'borrowed' Zeiss glasses would he please ensure that he had such a pair in his possession – with matching case.

'Oh yes,' he replied, 'and I suppose you would like your name inscribed in gold on the outside flap as well.'

'Very funny,' I said drily, but adding as an afterthought, 'Come to think of it though, if you *did* just happen to come across a second-hand pair with the same initials as mine that would certainly help things along!'

'F.O. Francis!' he exclaimed. 'What a fantasist! You can forget the initials but I might be able to pick up a pair of the sort you want. I've got a couple of contacts who owe me a favour or two...' What contacts and what favours I did not ask. But I thanked him gratefully, and not wanting to linger was about to ring off when he said smoothly, 'Of course, there's more to all this than meets the eye. I always said you were a dark horse – in your way, that is. As they say, it takes one to know–'

I replaced the receiver and sat crossly on the hall chair. 'Typical of Nicholas,' I brooded, 'always did have a sneaky mind!' Nevertheless I was cheered by his promise of help and felt that a small celebration was in order. The church organ beckoned.

Tapsell, its guard dog, was attending an

organists' jamboree down in Winchester and would not be back until the following day, and thus the coast was clear for me to indulge to my heart's content. Tapsell's pride in his musical talents is matched only by the obsessiveness with which he discharges his custodial duties. Thus when not in use the organ is resolutely locked and its key kept in a small box (also locked) in the vestry. I of course have the keys both to the vestry and to the box; so breaching Tapsell's barriers presented no difficulty.

I sat down at the instrument, rolled up my sleeves and commenced my flawed but enthusiastic repertoire. A happy hour was spent maiming Handel, the Bachs, Widor, and ending up with my special, though perforce rather lugubrious, version of 'Tea For Two'. It was at this point that I caught sight of Miss Dalrymple prowling in a side aisle – a sighting that made me stumble in what was to have been a superlative glissando. But this was only a passing hiccup for I recalled that Miss Dalrymple was tone-deaf and incapable of distinguishing Beethoven from Black Bottom. Besides, judging from her crouching gait she was clearly on one of her gum-seeking missions and far too intent to register either the music or the player.

I continued for another ten minutes and then, pleased with my performance and buoyed by its sense of the illicit, returned home in moderately good spirits. There was nothing pressing to attend to that evening, no more than usual at any rate, and I decided to have an early night with a good book. The books in my study are shelved in reproachful disorder for I had never got around to classifying them after the move from Bermondsey. My fingers hovered quizzically between the adjacent spines of Machiavelli and Mickey Spillane. Both are a good read, but in the end I went for the *Lives of the Saints*.

The next morning I awoke refreshed but was irritated to discover the organ key still in my jacket pocket. I was about to return it to the vestry when the post arrived and I was diverted by an unwelcome letter. It was from Violet Pond, demanding that I be at home the following day to receive her and a couple of her cousins to 'give further thought to Mother's will'. I thought the woman had an infernal cheek, and certainly did not relish the prospect of family reinforcements. One specimen of Pond-life was quite enough. I rather wished that Primrose was with me. She has an awesome capacity for repulsing the unlovely and uninvited.

As I reread the letter and debated what to do, the telephone rang. It was Tapsell returned from Winchester and in a state of outrage.

'Some bugger's swiped the key to the organ...' he began.

'Well, this bugger hasn't,' I snapped, fingering the key in my pocket and putting down the receiver. It occurred to me afterwards that perhaps I had been a little terse. Still, Tapsell did not have to contend with Violet Pond and her cohorts. Surely in the circumstances I might be forgiven for sounding a mite fragile. Later that morning I saw Mrs Tapsell in the town and made a point of giving her a cheery wave. It was not reciprocated.

I also encountered the whippet. He was mooching along on his own, sallow face puckered as he struggled to roll a cigarette. There was a keen wind blowing and I had already noticed two papers flutter to the ground. He seemed so absorbed in the manoeuvre that at first I thought he had not seen me – but of course he had. Not much escapes Samson's questing eye. He looked up, pocketed his tobacco tin and nodded unsmilingly.

I was eager to know whether contact had been made with Nicholas but was loath to ask for fear of appearing unduly concerned. An air of careless nonchalance was surely the best approach. Thus I bade him good morning, said a couple of words about the weather and prepared to stroll on but he stopped me.

'We've checked your story.'

I resented the term 'story' but said lightly, 'Oh yes,' and waited for him to elaborate.

'Yes, the Sussex police saw your friend Mr Ingaza and they are satisfied he had the binoculars.' (That was a relief!) He sounded disappointed.

'Well, naturally they are satisfied. I had already told you he borrowed them.'

'Yes,' he replied sceptically, 'you did *tell* us.' I was glad to see that he looked gloomy but was less glad when he suddenly brightened and said with some relish, 'Your friend, this Mr Nicholas Ingaza, he's got form, hasn't he? He's been inside.'

Adopting one of my colder tones I said that I could not see what on earth that had to do with it. And in any case it had all happened years ago and was due to an entirely personal lapse.

'Buggery generally is ... personal, I mean.

Training to be a parson, wasn't he? Just goes to show, can't trust anybody these days!' And he had the gall to give a low whistle and grin sardonically.

I was incensed by his sly impertinence and for once felt defensive of Nicholas – and indeed of the Church. My instinct was to tell him that in my opinion he was a short-arsed pusillanimous little worm deserving the attentions of the garden spade. However, self-preservation prevailed. At all costs I could not afford to antagonize *Them*. Instead I had to be satisfied with saying in a silky vicar voice that I thought his manners could do with a polish and I trusted that the Chief Constable, one of my most zealous parishioners, would not hold such breach against him. It wasn't very good but in the circumstances the best I could manage, and I strolled off with what I liked to think was an air of languid indifference.

28

The Vicar's Version

I wasn't looking forward to the day. The prospect of her visit hung like a pall and despite rising early I could not throw off its dreary weight. Fortunately Savage was coming round that morning with more of his wife's homemade cakes. I say 'fortunately' because I find his company both convivial and soothing. He harbours no expectations and makes no demands, and has a kind of cheery cynicism that does wonders for the spirit. I grumbled to him about Violet Pond's impending visit.

'Just don't know what to do,' I said morosely.

He thought and then said brightly, 'Has she got a hat?'

'How should I know! What's that to do with it?'

'Well, you see, if she's got a hat you could tell her you liked it. They always enjoy that sort of thing.'

'But I wouldn't.'

'Wouldn't what?'

'Like her hat.'

'That doesn't matter – just tell her you like it and she'll be eating out of your hand. It works a treat with my wife.'

Having already witnessed Violet Pond consuming a cream bun, I did not find the prospect of her eating out of my hand a happy one and told him as much.

'Your language is getting a bit ripe these days, isn't it, vicar!' he chuckled. I apologized, explaining that I had been under rather a strain recently, and hoped I hadn't given offence.

'Good Lord, no! After all, what's a few imprecations between friends!' I was comforted by that – not so much because he hadn't taken offence but rather by the suggestion of friendship. It was nice to know that there was at least somebody on my side.

I was also struck by his reference to Mrs Savage and the hat-trick. 'If you don't mind my asking, since your eyesight's a bit dodgy how are you able to compliment her on what she is wearing? I mean ... are you able to see a bit of it perhaps?'

'Oh no. Blind as a bat I am!' he said cheerfully. 'But that makes no difference. Now you and I might apply logic to the situation, but *they* don't, not where their vanity's concerned. Tell 'em they're wearing a nice hat and they'll believe you even if you had a paper bag over your head. Or if they did, for that matter! It's all a question of female psychology,' he declared confidently.

I know very little of female psychology, and reflected that had I known more perhaps Elizabeth Fotherington would yet be alive. However, such musings were by the way: the immediate problem was how to fend off her daughter. I thanked Savage for his advice and told him I would let him know how I got on.

Mrs Pond arrived at twelve o'clock accompanied not by two strapping male kinsmen as I had nervously expected, but by a diminutive woman wearing drooping grey tweeds, grey stockings and a shrivelled look. She was introduced vaguely as 'a cousin of mine' but no name was ascribed.

Waving aside offers of sherry, Violet Pond launched into yet another of her baleful monologues. It differed little from the first time around except that now it was punctuated by expectant looks at the cousin, who quite obviously had lost the plot before it began and was heavily engrossed in examining her shoelaces. Occasionally the head would lift and a vacant nod be delivered. Other than that she contributed nothing; and unless she had a microphone up her sleeve or was a white witch silently casting spells on her cousin's persecutor, her presence seemed to have no obvious function.

Yet again Mrs Pond appealed to my better nature, stressing as she had done in the press interview her mother's inability to grasp the importance of family finance. I smiled sympathetically but unhelpfully. She droned on about the hardships of being 'a woman alone' (in fact, gossip had it that she had wrested a more than adequate pay-off from her erstwhile husband), and I started to fidget and longed for a cigarette. Then she brought Clinker into it.

'You do know that I've approached your bishop, I suppose?'

'Really?' I asked in surprise. Certainly he had referred to the matter but I had assumed he had gained his knowledge from newspaper reports and the diocesan grapevine. I didn't realize she had made a direct appeal.

'Yes, really,' she snapped. Then she added acidly, 'Not that he's been much use, a more fatuous prelate I have yet to encounter. All he would do was um and ah and burble on about Molehill being in a safe pair of hands. I can hardly imagine he meant yours... What do *you* think?' she barked to her silent companion. The latter, increasingly riveted by the shoelaces, remained mute.

Mrs Pond leaned forward, and as if I had become her ally against Clinker exclaimed, 'Do you know, the third time I telephoned him – just when I was about to explain the illegality of that codicil, some appalling woman with a voice like a cannon interrupted and had the brass neck to tell me to get off the line! Can't think who it was – his minder presumably!'

'His wife actually,' I murmured, recognizing the style and giving the ghastly Gladys her due marks.

'Well, wife or not, it isn't the sort of response you expect from the Bishop's Palace. I shall take the matter higher up. *Much* higher – make no mistake!' I felt a spasm of schadenfreude, wondering whether Fisher could possibly conceive what was brewing up for him.

Then, feeling that it was time I tried to defuse things, I cut her short by playing what I fondly imagined to be my trump card: a résumé of the charitable causes already earmarked for my bequest. She was unimpressed, observing that had pensioners made proper provision for themselves during their working lives there would be no need to waste money on Christmas bun-fights. As to the Community Hall – she knew all about Brown Owls and Cub leaders from the pages of the *News of the World* and had no wish to see her mother's money being used in that particular direction! Reluctant to add fuel to flame I resisted pointing out that it was my money and not her mother's. Instead I enthused about my idea of an Elizabeth Fotherington Memorial Prize, thinking that this at least would meet with her approval. Not a bit of it. Shooting me a look of excoriating scorn she declared that her mother's musical knowledge had been so ludicrously abysmal that to link her name with a choral prize would be an act of gross idiocy.

I sighed. We seemed to have reached an impasse, perhaps a suitable moment to ask her to leave. As I debated this my eye fell upon the small table next to her chair. She had placed her gloves there and a rather grubby knitted item which at first I took to be a string shopping-bag. And then I realized that it was not a bag but a form of crumpled headgear. Savage and his vaunted knowledge of female psychology came to mind. I would jolly well put it to the test!

Clearing my throat I said winningly, 'What a fetching beret you have, Mrs Pond – and in such a subtle colour too!' (I was rather proud of that last bit, feeling it showed a discerning eye.)

She glared suspiciously, but before she could make any response there was a violent movement from the hitherto passive cousin who leapt to her feet and in a voice of sparrow glee cried, 'You see, Violet – at *least* the vicar appreciates my efforts!' Beaming down at me from her short height, she picked the thing up and thrust it under my nose.

'I use a special wool twine that's water-proof – waxed, you know – they sell it in Hodge & Bewley... And then of course the stitching is my own invention, a knack I developed as a girl. Quite a little trademark you might say! People find it fascinating.' (I looked duly fascinated). She continued: 'I am so glad you like the colour. Grey is such a serviceable shade, it goes with anything – though I have been thinking of branching out into khaki. Rather a daring departure! What do *you* think, Mr Oughterard?'

I considered the matter. 'I think you should stick to grey. Khaki is a tinge masculine whereas grey is softer and suits all complexions.'

'Oh yes, vicar,' she squeaked, 'my views exactly. What an encouragement – I shall commence a new batch immediately!' Smiling blissfully she returned the limp article to Violet Pond, who with a face of thunder rammed it into her handbag and lumbered to her feet.

'Well, that's it,' she exploded. 'That is *it!* I've had enough... Look what I'm up against! Swamped by a sea of imbeciles: first Mother, then the solicitors, a weak-kneed bishop, an addled cousin – and now to cap it all, a plundering clergyman who thinks he's Hardy Amies!' Seizing the Unnamed by her arm she dragged her protesting to the door and out on to the path. I watched as they made their disputing way to the gate. While Cousin Violet struggled to wrench it open the Unnamed looked back and gave me a perky wave.

After they had gone I strode into the kitchen, scooped up Maurice, collared Bouncer and took them off to the graveyard where the three of us sat on one of the larger tombs enjoying the sun and the blessed silence. I smoked, Maurice stalked, Bouncer played. Had a corner been turned? I wondered.

29

The Vicar's Version

The snag with turning corners is that you have no guarantee of what lies round the bend. 'That when ye think all danger for to pass/Ware the lizard lieth lurking in the grass,' warned the Tudor poet John Skelton. And that afternoon a particularly sneaky one lay coiled beneath the graveyard's sprawling tussocks. As I leant against the tombstone watching my smoke-rings spiral lazily into the trees, the elusive detail which for the past few weeks had been nagging away at the back of my mind suddenly thrust itself into sharp focus: my gold cigarette lighter with its elegantly engraved gothic initials.

At the time its loss had been an annoyance but my attention had been absorbed by weightier issues and I had given only cursory thought to its whereabouts. Now, however, it occurred to me that the thing lay not in Rummage's grasping pocket but more than likely in the undergrowth of Foxford Wood. I could not be sure of course, a mere conjecture, but neither could I banish the growing sense of unease. As the days passed conjecture turned to certainty and every time I lit a cigarette the match seemed to rebuke me with its loss. There was no doubt about it: the thing was there in the wood, in the place where it must have slipped from my pocket when I was lugging that dreadful burden. I could see the very spot – the kink in the path where it veered sharply to the right, the little mound of chalky broken stones, the sprawling spindle-berry brushing the bracken; and then a few yards on, the canopy of hawthorn under which she had been so carefully stowed. I shut my eyes, bludgeoned by memory, stunned by the sudden pressing reality of it all.

Clearly that was where the lighter lay – brazenly exposed for all to see! Except, of course, they *hadn't* seen it. According to the newspapers the spot had yielded nothing to the police investigation, and while March and Samson had been obsessed with the matter of the binoculars there had certainly been no reference to a cigarette lighter. Caught perhaps in a knot of bracken, shielded by a clod of earth, somehow it had escaped the searchers' eyes; had lain there – did lie – protected by the undergrowth, lost and secret.

Such thoughts helped at least to disperse the panic if not the underlying anxiety. But to some extent this latter I could control by pursuing the parochial round and busying myself in matters more mundane. Then of course the blow was struck...

As I walked home one afternoon from visiting a parishioner I met Savage tapping his way along the pavement with his bag of tuning tools slung over his shoulder. Normally an encounter with Savage leaves me considerably refreshed, but not this time. He was whistling cheerfully but unmelodiously and I couldn't help thinking that for a man of his profession he displayed a curious lack of rhythm. Indeed I said something to that effect as we drew level and he grinned good-naturedly, observing that we couldn't all be clerical Liberaces and that if I really wanted to hear something good he would teach me how to beat up the drums one day. He also said something else, something which froze my marrow.

'They're going to do that wood again, you know.'

'What do you mean "do it"? Who?'

'The police. They've got to do another search of the murder scene in Foxwood

Wood. I've got a nephew in the Force and according to him old man March copped it from some senior rankers for not doing the job properly first time round. Apparently he's not coming up with the goods quick enough. Anyway they're going to give it another going over, and with dogs this time.'

Yes, I thought, like swine rooting for golden truffles. And in my mind's eye I saw a triumphant dog-handler patting his charge and proudly displaying the trophy to his admiring colleagues.

'Well,' I said casually, 'let's hope they do better this time. When will it happen?'

'Don't know,' he replied, 'soon I suppose. It'll have to be daylight of course – tomorrow morning maybe... Anyway, must be off now, vicar. Just one more job then home to Mrs Savage. She's in one of her fragile moods and I'll have to pussy-foot around a bit – get her to read out a few clues perhaps.' And with a chuckle he resumed his tuneless whistling and sauntered off.

When I got home I was so tense I could hardly breathe, and sat on the stairs head in hands and my mind gripped alternately by whirling fears and frozen paralysis. The dog pottered out from the sitting room, and seeing me there in my agitated state stopped abruptly and stared hard. He ambled into the kitchen and returned with something in his mouth, a macerated biscuit which he deposited at my feet. I was touched by the gesture, gave him a cursory pat but declined the offer. I sat on, imagining the worst and gearing myself to act – for action was certainly required! I would go back to the wood. It was a prospect I hardly relished but if there was even the merest chance of finding the thing before *They* did then it would have to be done.

The decision made, I was able to confront the situation in a calmer light, but I was troubled by the obvious risk. Apart from a natural reluctance to retrace my former footsteps there was also the question of security. At the time of the event I had been relieved not to have met anyone either going to or coming from the wood; and thus, as far as I knew, my movements that morning had gone unnoticed. But one could never be entirely sure. Memory is a curious thing and often what is overlooked at the time can be resurrected long afterwards by the stimulus of a chance sighting or event. Crime reconstructions are based precisely on that fact. Supposing there were someone out there whose buried memory of that day was suddenly rekindled by seeing me once more traipsing across the meadow? A further thought nagged me – the popularly held belief that the criminal invariably returns to the scene of the crime. True or not, at least by *not* going back I had up to now made myself safe from that particular suspicion.

Such caution was fine in principle: in practice the new developments forced my hand and I should have to chance it. The difficulty lay in how to reduce the possibility of being seen while still having enough light to look for the damn thing! Eager though I was to start the search immediately, the best time surely would be early evening: dusk with people at supper, children curfewed.

Thus resolved, I tried to spend the next couple of hours checking the week's hymn list and making desultory forays into the crossword. I thought a little piano practice might help pass the time but it didn't. My fingers were leaden, brain distracted. Instead I shut the lid and poured a whisky and could have done with another but resisted, knowing that the evening's project would require all my faculties.

At last, judging the time to be about right I put on a dark jacket and low peaked cap, pocketed a small torch and went to open the back door. I was waylaid by Bouncer clearly intent on coming with me. He could have been useful, for a person walking a dog is commonplace and somehow innocuous, whereas the sight of a solitary man roaming the woods at twilight might be remarked. However, I decided against it. Bouncer's company is enlivening but disruptive and he would only impede and complicate matters.

With head down and keeping close to the hedge I skirted the field and moved rapidly towards the camouflage of the trees. As I walked I recalled wryly the last time I had come this way. Then it had been a bright June morning, dew on the grass, the leaves green and fresh, birds chattering; and despite Elizabeth's awful pursuit I had been, relatively speaking, a free man. Now it was a late September evening with shadows lengthening, leaves turning, a hint of autumnal dankness touching the air and weighing on my spirit – and I was far from free.

The moment I entered the wood the absurdity of the situation struck me. The place was darker than I had expected, the mellow light of the fields replaced by an oppressive gloaming, and the undergrowth so much denser than I had remembered. Patently it was a fool's errand: there wasn't a hope in hell of finding the thing and I cursed my stupidity for even contemplating the idea. I was about to retreat but the image of those police dogs sniffing around at the scene, perhaps in only a few hours' time, was intolerable. And so, driven by desperation, I pressed on. To buoy things up I tried to persuade myself that the task would be less impossible than I thought. After all, I could recall the exact spot where the deed had occurred, and dragging the body to the hawthorn tree had been a matter of a mere few yards. It was only in that small area that I had engaged in the sort of strenuous activity which would have caused the lighter to slip from my pocket. A really intensive search of that confined patch might just do the trick. Perhaps for once luck would be on my side. Stranger things had happened.

In fact, as things turned out the matter remained untested: I never reached the spot. For something occurred which drove the plan, rational or otherwise, completely from my mind.

As I moved further in amongst the trees the light receded and I had glimpses of the rising moon gliding wanly above the entangled branches. The stillness which on that

June day had seemed so soothing now felt alien; and when as before the sudden bark of a roebuck broke the silence I had a terrible sense of déjà vu and felt the creature was somehow mocking my presence. I quickened my step, eager to reach the place before the light really failed. And then, just as I had discerned the heap of broken stones at the curve of the path, there was a sound of loud scrabblings coming from the bushes to my left. At first I assumed it was a pheasant or possibly a fox but the noise continued and seemed to be accompanied by faint snortings. Badgers.

I crept forward carefully, hoping to have a sighting of Brock with his lady and brood, and camouflaging myself behind a convenient tree trunk peered stealthily into the little clearing...What I saw was neither Brock nor his lady – but a substantial pair of lunging naked buttocks.

I stood rooted with incredulity as the motion accelerated and the snortings got louder; and even in my shock I remember being fascinated by the way the moon cast a sort of unearthly pallor upon the heaving fundament giving it a halo-like glow. However, my absorption was short-lived for with a muffled squeal a woman's voice cried,

'Stop! Stop! Bloody hell, it's the vicar!'

Her escort did as he was bid. And as he scrambled to his feet, cursing and hauling up his trousers, I saw that the joy-rider was Tapsell. I also observed that he was still wearing his bicycle clips. We stared at each other in mutual horror. And then with possibly even greater horror I realized that his companion-in-arms was Mavis Briggs' sworn enemy, Edith Hopgarden.

'What the hell are you doing here?' Tapsell snarled. 'You can't go around snooping on people like this, creeping up on them from behind trees. There's a word for that sort of thing, you know. It's disgraceful. It's not right!'

I was tempted to point out that he was not exactly in the best position to talk of others' disgrace, but instead sought desperately for something to explain my apparently furtive presence. I cleared my throat.

'Moths,' I said. 'I was looking for moths.'

'Looking for moths? What are you talking about?' he cried. 'What in God's name do you want moths for?'

'Well, you see, I do a bit of collecting – dabble in lepidoptery and the evening is the best time for them. You know, the Elephant Hawk, the Garden Tiger, the Lesser Swallow

Prominent...' (I knew nothing about these but had heard their names intoned by our botany master at prep school.) Actually I was rather pleased with this feat of memory but Tapsell seemed unimpressed and went blustering on, saying that he didn't care what I dabbled in and was buggered if he was going to be spied upon by some sodding busybody, vicar or no. I was rather nettled by this outburst and in any case it was starting to turn chilly, so thinking I might exploit the moral advantage I murmured quietly that that was not the sort of language I expected to hear from my church organist and that if he had any sense he would pedal straight home to Mrs Tapsell who might be a trifle surprised were she to learn of his current whereabouts. I added graciously that naturally the matter need never be referred to again.

As hoped, this mild admonition had the desired effect and he sobered somewhat. The same could not be said for Edith Hopgarden who, hitherto silent, now launched into a bout of prolonged wailing.

'Oh God – you've set her off now!' exclaimed Tapsell. 'That's all I need!' And grabbing the wretched Edith by the wrist he dragged her past me, and the two of them disappeared into the darkness presumably in the direction of one or both of their abandoned bicycles.

I walked home thoughtfully and considerably lighter in spirit. Memory can play embarrassing tricks, and even now I can rarely see a moth of any category without some idiot's defenceless posterior looming into my mind.

30

The Vicar's Version

They came a third time, turning up out of the blue and putting me in a flat spin. It was late afternoon and I was in the middle of grappling with the Sunday School rota. This was not usually my task but Edith Hopgarden who was technically responsible had had one of her turns (manufactured I suspect in vengeance for the wood incident), and the prospect of substituting Mavis Briggs as the arch controller had been too awful to contemplate.

As they came to the door I was convinced

that it was to confront me with that golden piece of evidence. In fact nothing was said about the lighter at all. Instead March produced from his raincoat pocket a small yellow notebook and put it on the table.

'That's her diary,' he announced. 'You're in it.' There was a silence, and my stomach lurched.

'Am I?' I said weakly.

'Yes, you're mentioned a number of times. Seems you saw her quite often.' (Too damn often! I thought).

'No more than many of my parishioners,' I replied evenly. 'One is expected to be sociable, it goes with the job.' And then as casually as I could, 'May I ask what form the references take?'

'Oh, nothing *compromising*,' interrupted Samson snidely, '–nothing to worry about, I should say.' And he gave a brazen grin.

'It never crossed my mind there would be anything to worry about,' I lied drily.

March frowned at Samson, cleared his throat and started to flip through the pages.

'They're just social engagements. For example – "April 2nd, Vicar for lunch; April 7th, Francis returns library book; April 10th, Help Francis with his pruning." (Yes, I recalled, a ghastly afternoon!) "'May 4th,

Tea at the vicarage; May 18th, Take rhubarb to Francis"... That sort of thing. But the point is, because she saw you so regularly I thought perhaps you could help us with this particular entry. It doesn't seem to tie up with anything else in the diary. A bit puzzling really. Maybe you can suggest something...'

He passed the book over to me with a page turned down and dated June 4th. It read as follows: 'Really, things impossible. So frustrating! Something definite must be done. Will have to speak out. Dangerous of course but a risk worth taking. Will watch and wait and use the first opportunity. Who knows – kill or cure!!'

Even as I read the words those girlish breathy tones echoed in my ear. 'Well,' I remarked, 'I cannot imagine what she was talking about but presumably she didn't get her cure.' And then fearing that sounded a trifle facetious, added quickly, 'Poor lady!'

March looked thoughtful. 'She was obviously concerned about something – or somebody. What was the risk, and what were the "things"?'

'Perhaps she was worried about her health,' I suggested helpfully. This "kill or cure" bit ... maybe she was thinking about a new treatment.'

'Treatment for what?' asked Samson sniffing loudly. The term 'manic fixation' came to mind but I said nothing.

'It's a thought, you know,' said March, turning to Samson. 'The Reverend might just have something there. We'll check the medical records anyway, otherwise we could find ourselves barking up the wrong tree. Wouldn't want that, would we?' And he gave me a slow, indulgent smile.

Suddenly I saw it. Oh my God, I thought, he's humouring me! Playing me along, spinning out yards of rope. The diary business was a red herring, some device to keep me talking while they, like her, would watch and wait... I began to feel the familiar signs of panic welling up: the tight chest, the cold hands. Any moment they were going to drop their bombshell and I knew exactly what it would be: the lighter. They were going to produce the bastard lighter! Already I seemed to hear March's wooden voice intoning, 'F.O. – your initials, are they not, Mr Oughterard? Quite a coincidence really, that we should find this just where the body was...' And I stared paralysed as he turned back frowning to the diary.

An appalling sound came from the hall: a demonic wail of crazed incandescent fury. It was Maurice. He gets like that sometimes. Obviously Bouncer had overstepped the mark again. The next instant, amidst a vortex of howls and shrieks, the dog flung himself through the doorway pursued by the raging Maurice. Stunned by the suddenness of their entry we watched helplessly as Nature red in tooth and claw played out its merry hell within the narrow confines of my sitting room. Impervious to human presence, dog and cat rampaged around our feet screeching and snarling in an ecstasy of foaming wrath. The sight was awesome, the noise excruciating. Armageddon had come upon us and we were ill prepared.

'Christ!' yelped the whippet as Maurice, hissing like a fiend, catapulted between his knees and leaped on to the curtain. There he swung gibbon-like, spitting oaths at Bouncer who, prancing wildly below, careered into the music stool and sent it scudding along the floor. As it fell the lid shot back on its ratchet, and crashing on to the boards there cascaded an avalanche of foul, jaundiced, rancid old bones...

The three of us stared down in fascinated disbelief. The silence was total. But even in my shock I registered the cat slinking from the room and that Bouncer was meekly and unaccountably engrossed in something outside the window. And then March stepped forward, and stooping down picked from the charnel heap a small gold object.

'F.O. – your initials, are they not, Mr Oughterard? Unusual place to keep a cigarette lighter.'

'Or bones, for that matter!' observed the whippet indignantly. Then with a gasp he cried, 'My God, there's a dead mouse there too!' And there was: a fieldmouse – small, fawn, mangled. They looked at each other and then at me. I suddenly felt quite ill and had to sit down abruptly.

'You don't look well, sir,' observed March kindly.

'No,' I answered faintly, 'I don't think I am...' He instructed Samson to fetch a glass of water which the latter thrust at me with an ill grace. As I sipped I gazed in mesmerized wonder at the bones strewn around my feet. Bouncer was still riveted by whatever was going on in the garden and appeared oblivious to the scene within the room. I realized that somehow the bones must have arrived by his agency, that the dog had carried them there and effected a quasi-burial. As to the cigarette lighter, the more I pondered its presence, the more peculiar I felt.

I took a few more sips, and then in as matter-of-fact a voice as I could muster said, 'The dog is awful with his bones, you know, leaves them everywhere. So dangerous! I try to throw them away but he gets upset and raids the dustbins. It's easier just to plonk them into the music stool where he can get at them when he wants.'

'Ah,' said March slowly, 'and you plonk your gold lighter there too, do you, with the bones?'

'Must have scooped it up with a couple of them by mistake,' I mumbled. 'Been looking for it for ages...'

There was a silence while they continued to gaze at me. And then March said, 'We'll be off now, sir. If you don't mind me saying, you look a bit pale. Been overdoing it, I expect. If I were you I'd take a nap.' They moved to the front door and let themselves out.

As they walked down the path I saw Samson glance back at the house, and then turning to his companion tap his forehead in a way that was quite unmistakable. I retired to bed.

31

The Cat's Memoir

During the fracas with the bones I made a hasty exit to the garden and thence to the graveyard where I spent a congenial hour playing with the sparrows. I was just on my way back to the house, curious to see how things were progressing, when I was met by Bouncer. He came trundling along sniffing the air and wearing quite an agreeable expression.

'Ah, glad I've found you,' he said cheerfully, 'thought we ought to chew things over, have a bit of a bow-wow.' I refrained from correcting him, feeling there had been quite enough excitement for one day, and said I thought it a very sensible idea. He beamed.

'I say, that was a good dust-up, wasn't it!' he exclaimed. 'We haven't had one like that for ages – blows the cobwebs away, you might say!'

'*You* might say,' I replied, 'but personally I

am not in the habit of festooning myself in cobwebs.'

'No, but you enjoy a good romp though, don't you, Maurice!' I acknowledged that as romps go it had indeed been invigorating. We sat down in the lee of a tombstone and began the bow-wow.

I told him I wanted a full account of how things had gone in my absence. He said I hadn't missed much: that F.O. had continued to sit on the chair pale and twitching, that the detectives had hovered around for a while clearing their throats and staring at the bones and had then sloped off muttering. He added that the puny one, Samson, kept tapping his forehead as he walked down the path.

'Why do you think he was doing that, Maurice? Trying to bag a flea?' I explained to him that it was a constant habit with humans, that they did it whenever they thought that one of their kind was unhinged – which was fairly often.

'Ah, well ... yes, I see,' he replied. He then volunteered further information for which I was quite unprepared.

'Mind you, they didn't like the mouse much!'

'What mouse?'

'You know, the dead one that was in there.' I had no idea what he was talking about and said as much.

'You can't have noticed. Too many bones around, I suppose. It was one of yours actually.'

I glared at him. 'One of *mine!* What do you mean? You don't imagine I would put my spoils into your disgusting piano stool!'

'No,' he grinned, 'but O'Shaughnessy did.' This was getting beyond a joke and I told him so sharply.

'Well, *we* thought it was funny,' he said. 'O'Shaughnessy found it behind the kitchen cupboard and said we might as well shove it in along with the lighter. He said perhaps you'd miss it and that'd set the cat among the pigeons all right!' He chortled inanely and shot me a furtive look from under his fringe. I decided that a cool disdain was the best response, and apart from remarking that O'Shaughnessy was getting too big for his collar did not pursue the matter.

We then went on to review the general situation. 'On the whole,' Bouncer observed thoughtfully, 'I don't think those police are getting very far with the vicar. I mean, it's not as if they've got proof of anything.' I agreed, saying that thanks to our alacrity and sleight-of-paw with the lighter, they had got very little to go on, particularly as F.O. had shown enough wit to sort out the binocular business.

He looked at me steadily and then said quietly, 'It was me that buried the lighter in the first place, and *me* that brought it back safely to the house and buried it in the stool.'

'*With* O'Shaughnessy's assistance,' I corrected him quickly. 'And frankly if I hadn't been there to direct operations that thing would still be in the wood today, or more likely with the police forensic people. Kindly remember that!' He muttered something unintelligible into his beard which I didn't quite catch though it sounded a little like 'Oh get off your broomstick!', but I don't suppose it was.

'What is he doing now?' I enquired.

'Gone to bed.'

'He seems to make a habit of that!'

'Only place he can get peace and quiet. Like me with my crypt.'

I nodded. 'Yes, that's been the problem all along. A bit of peace and quiet – it's the only thing he wants really. He was all right until that wretched mistress of mine got him in her sights!'

'Well,' said Bouncer, 'not *quite* all right, but nearly.'

We thought about that for a while. And then he said, 'You know, Maurice, we ought to try being very good for a time. Sort of make it easy for him.'

'Fat chance of that,' I retorted, 'when you and that asinine setter go about putting decapitated mice into his piano stool!' He obviously thought that was hugely funny and started to roll about snorting and gurgling and drumming his hind legs on the grass. I left him to it, and glad to escape those lunatic sounds set off on my nightly patrol.

32

The Vicar's Version

When I woke it was the middle of the night, and I lay staring into the gloom listening to an owl and the steady ticking of the landing clock. At first, dragged from sleep my mind was blank, and for perhaps one precious minute I savoured the comfort of the bed and the peace of the embalming dark. Then of course officious memory came surging back and I relived the events of the afternoon.

How could he have carried so many bones! When did he do it? How long had they been there? (Some time presumably, judging from their appearance!) How often did he visit the stool? And what about that disgusting mouse? I dwelled on these questions at length because in this way I could delay confronting the real one: the crucial one, the one about the lighter. I started to persuade myself that it must have been Rummage after all, that he had found it and for some reason best known to himself had deposited it in the stool. But even as I clutched at this feeble straw I knew it wasn't so. Try as I might to think otherwise, that lighter had not been in my pocket on my return from Foxford Wood; it *had* been there when I went.

Yet again I mentally retraced my steps there and back; recalled the atmosphere of the wood, the mossy scent which had stifled my desire to smoke; my left hand fumbling in my trouser pocket for the cigarettes, feeling the lighter there, rejecting it in favour of the peppermints. After the incident itself I had been in such a trance that at the time nothing had impinged. But in retrospect the memory of that return journey took on a harrowing clarity. Between arrival in the wood and departure from it my mood had changed. And as I now recalled only too well, by the time I was once more in the fields I *had* wanted to smoke – and had been frustrated by lack of means. There was no doubt about it: that lighter with its distinctively engraved initials had fallen out of my pocket somewhere close to the main path, probably at what had been her very hiding place. Yes, it was definitely as I had originally feared! So how in God's name had it reached the piano stool?

Lying there wrestling with these images I concluded that there might be a perfectly simple explanation: I was going gently but irrevocably mad. Perhaps I had been responsible for filling the piano stool with those bones. And shocked by the Tapsell episode, had I perhaps made some midnight somnambulation back to the wood intent on completing unfinished business, and finding the lighter placed it carefully in its musical burial chamber? (Propitiation to the gods perhaps?) Surely an event such as I had perpetrated those three months ago would be enough to turn anyone's mind! I contemplated this possibility with a mixture of comfort and apprehension. Comfort to know that at least here was a perfectly logical explanation; but worry to think that having escaped the genteel ennui of St Chad's I was already marked down for another place of asylum in which to end my muddled days.

Further cogitations resolved nothing. I listened to the church clock strike the half-hour, and unable to stand the tensions any longer got out of bed and padded downstairs to make some tea. Waiting for the kettle to boil I went to fetch the crossword from the sitting room. Perhaps that would induce a little sanity. I began to move towards the table and promptly stubbed my toe on a bone. The things lay splayed out like some broken fossilized fan ('fragments shored against my ruins'?). Cursing, I started to shovel them to one side, and then spotted the cigarette lighter on the arm of the chair where March had left it. Hesitantly and with a sense of awe I picked it up, gave it a quick polish on my pyjama sleeve and slipped it into the top pocket. My toe was throbbing and had started to bleed on to the carpet. Bloody dog.

In fact in the kitchen Bouncer looked as good as gold. Despite my crashing about he lay curled up in his basket beside the boiler seemingly fast asleep. Not much of a guard, I thought bitterly. I sipped the tea and turned my waning wits to the crossword. Few of the clues looked accessible and I thought enviously of Savage's talents in that sphere. As I wrestled with a set of conundrums unconnected with the present problem, reason gradually began to return. I drank more tea and at last found a clue which gave some hope of a solution. Five across, ten letters: 'First of September's gone, but Nora's tum is still a tender place.' I pondered and then grabbed the pencil, and feeling rather pleased with myself wrote in S-A-N-A-T-O-R-I-U-M. Instantly pleasure vanished, and with a groan I stumbled back to bed.

The next day was surprisingly congenial. With the help of breakfast the travails of the night faded somewhat and I was able to establish a perspective. Despite the embarrassment of the previous day's events it was obvious that, by being in the piano stool rather than in Foxford Wood, the cigarette lighter had not caught the attention of March and Samson – at least not in any crucial way. If they thought me peculiar for housing my valuables amidst mice and marrow bones then that was their prerogative, but it hardly constituted proof of murder! And despite Reginald Bowler's tasteless allegation, nor did Elizabeth's frequent diary references. Thinking about this I felt much better. When all was said and done, salacious innuendo and an uncanny mystery were undoubtedly more manageable than a night (or far worse!) in the cells.

I celebrated this comforting thought with an extra slice of toast and Marmite. As I munched, the door pushed open and Maurice glided in. He sat down and proceeded to sleek his paws and examine his under parts. A minute later Bouncer appeared, looking I thought a trifle diffident; but he sloped across the kitchen, wagged his tail vaguely in my direction and lay down next to the cat. They projected an air of smug collusion which was slightly unsettling. Still, I mused, better to be unsettled by a dog and a cat than by the hangman's noose.

I spent the morning busying myself with correspondence and checking the proofs of the church magazine, and then in the afternoon set off to the parish hall to present the Sunday School prizes and help with the raffle. Once over the threshold I was immediately accosted by Mavis Briggs who came twittering up describing in lurid detail her plans for the 'Little Gems of Uplift'. She prevailed upon me to attend the event, or thought she had, and then to my surprise launched into a paean of praise about what she called my 'munificence'. It seemed my plans re the legacy had been leaked to the *Molehill Clarion* which was now fêting me as the saviour of the Brownies. Apparently they and the Wolf Cubs were already rehearsing a jolly jamboree in my honour!

I was flattered by the news and thought that at least a jamboree could be no worse than Mavis's uplifting poems and probably a lot better. Two minutes later Miss Dalrymple approached, bone-crunched my hand and in stentorian tones declared that 'Molehill's OAPs can consider themselves fearfully lucky!' I was a bit thrown by this and then of course remembered: their Christmas Party Fund. So that had got off the ground, had it? Could it be possible that I was becoming Molehill's Man of the Moment?

On the way home I bought the evening paper, curious to see what was being said about my 'munificence'. Settled with a gin and triumphantly producing the recovered lighter, I began to scan the pages. The article came up readily enough but what captured my interest much more was one in the adjacent column.

LOCAL FLASHER FOUND DEAD!

Robert Willy can no longer cause affront by his persistent appearances from behind the trees in Foxford Wood. The elderly tramp, scourge of respectable walkers for more than a decade, was found two nights ago dead in a ditch close to Holly Bush Meadow on the A281. He had obviously been drinking heavily, police reported, and his trousers were in their usual state of disarray. The young constable first called to view the body said that for a dead man he had looked quite cheerful.

The *Molehill Clarion* has long been of the opinion that Willy had a hand in the mysterious Fotherington case (in which it has to be said police investigation has been more than tardy). In the last few months his antics had grown increasingly bizarre, and a reliable witness from over the Berkshire border tells us that the last time she had the misfortune to encounter him he was most definitely carrying a noose and a hatchet. We urge the police to pursue this line of enquiry for the sooner the whole grisly affair can be resolved the sooner Molehill can resume its seemly business.

'Hear, hear!' I cried. 'I'm all for that!' The sooner the town became its seemly self again, the more likelihood I might eventually get some peace and quiet. I turned back to the other article and reflected that if I was being so universally approved perhaps I could sponsor the Memorial Prize after all. In spite of Violet Pond's scorn of her mother's musical ignorance I felt that, had she been available, the lady in question would have surely revelled in the tribute. Yes, I would see Tapsell and the choirmaster the very next day!

Time for a little turn at the piano; there hadn't been a chance for ages. Pausing only to check the inside of the stool, I sat down and prepared to play ... and then hesitated. Play what? Brahms, Scarlatti, Ellington? As I debated, for some reason Bishop Clinker came into my mind and without more ado I launched into a particularly lavish rendering of 'Knees Up Mother Brown'.

33

The Vicar's Version

In the circumstances I felt a bit diffident in approaching Tapsell about the Choral Prize. He seemed to have been absent for a few days but I had already had an unfortunate encounter with Edith Hopgarden. She was emerging from the vestry festooned in swathes of trailing ivy and autumn foliage, no doubt bent on completing the weekly flower arrangements before Mavis Briggs could get at them. And when I said genially that the woods afforded such splendid material at this time of year she went very red in the face, gave me a baleful glare and said that I should know if anyone.

I was glad to find that when Tapsell did appear his earlier temper had been replaced by a shifty deference, and neither he nor Jenkins the choirmaster raised any objection to my idea of a Fotherington choral event. Indeed they appeared quite approving of the project and nodded solemnly when I mooted the idea of a special anthem in commemoration of its namesake. It was arranged that a Parish Committee meeting be called and the plan thoroughly aired and put to the vote.

The meeting was well attended, the subject stirring considerable interest. Following a brief discussion the proposal itself was passed unanimously but after that the actual mechanics of the matter were treated to voluble debate. Someone (doubtless Mavis Briggs) made the bright suggestion that the text should be original, i.e. that the congregation be encouraged to submit their own compositions. I was doubtful about this but the idea was eagerly seized by the others and my tentative objections overruled. They did, however, graciously concede that since the anthem was my plan in the first place and the Memorial Prize funded by my donation, I should be the final arbiter in the selection process. This at least gave me a degree of control. But it also brought interminable tedium.

As I had feared, the literary offerings were not of the highest order and ranged from maundering banality to insufferable pretension. The best were honest but uninspired and I began seriously to regret ever proposing the thing. Needless to say Mavis Briggs produced a piece of execrable mawkishness remarkable even by her standards. I told her it would be wasted as an anthem and was crying out to be used as the grand finale to her 'Gems of Uplift'. She turned pink with pleasure and rushed away to pen more glutinous lines.

The most rhythmically robust was Miss Dalrymple's, the verses swinging along like boots on tarmac. However, since every third line contained the words 'wrath' or 'ire' I felt it to be a trifle repetitive. The injunctions to 'smite thine enemy' and 'throttle the foe' also featured quite strongly, and thus despite the several Hallelujahs it was not a poem to which I was personally drawn.

The more I read the more dispirited I became. If Elizabeth was to have her name up in lights in a Memorial Anthem then even she deserved better than this! Clearly it was time for me to exercise my clerical pre-rogative and cock a snook at democracy. Thus with unaccustomed firmness I explained to the committee that fascinating though the entries were none quite matched the exacting criteria required by an anthem, and I had therefore come to the conclusion that Elizabeth's name would best be served by a recognized poet from the great canon of English Literature.

'Which one?' barked Colonel Dawlish. Naturally I had not the least idea; but clearing my throat and assuming a knowledgeable expression, I said I had two or three clear possibilities in mind and would give them my decision the following day.

Wearisome hours were then spent trawling through library books and old anthologies desperately trying to find something not only intrinsically fitting but which would mollify the rejected and vindicate my judgement. Much whisky was consumed and I ran out of cigarettes.

Over breakfast next morning, exhausted but satisfied, I gave a reading to Maurice and Bouncer who were sitting patiently by the boiler. The text comprised lines from the seventeenth-century lyricist Robert Herrick, and went like this:

I sing of brooks, of blossoms, birds, and
  bowers:
Of April, May, of June, and July-flowers.
I sing of may-poles, hock-carts, wassails,
  wakes,
Of bride-grooms, brides, and of their
  bridal-cakes.

I write of youth, of love, and have access
By these, to sing of cleanly-wantonness.
I sing of dews, of rains, and piece by piece
Of balm, of oil, of spice, and amber-
    grease.
I sing of times trans-shifting; and I write
How roses first came red, and lilies white.
I write of groves, of twilights, and I sing
The court of Mab, and of the Fairy-King.
I write of Hell; I sing (and ever shall)
Of Heaven, and hope to have it after all.

I was pleased with my choice. The piece
had, I felt, the merits of brevity, simplicity,
beauty and joy; and in its concluding clause
surely expressed a hope as universal as one
was ever likely to find. If Colonel Dawlish or
anybody else imagined they could do better
then they could tootle off and kick a can.
This time I would not be overruled. It was
to be the text for her anthem.

34

The Cat's Memoir

'That was good, wasn't it?' said Bouncer.

'What?'

'What F.O. was burbling on about at breakfast.'

'Well, it may have been,' I said doubtfully, 'but you won't have understood it.'

'Yes I did!' he retorted truculently.

'Nonsense, the words would have escaped you.'

'Some did,' he conceded, 'but I liked the sound. It was very nice indeed.' He started to rattle his bowl, a habit he has when feeling particularly obstinate. 'What's it for anyway?'

I explained patiently that it was some musical thing that F.O. was putting on in memory of the lady of whom he had disposed.

'Quite right and proper,' he said solemnly.

There is an odd streak of piety in Bouncer which manifests itself at times when one is least prepared. I think it may be the result of his sojourn among the bones in the crypt. I cannot recall noticing it prior to his arrival there. However, he suddenly cocked his ears and with a broad grin said, 'Just as long as it doesn't have any bells in, it'll be all right, won't it, Maurice?' Clearly he was referring to my campanological aversion. I gave a haughty whisk of my tail and for a while silence reigned. Not for long.

'Maurice,' he said suddenly, 'why do you think he did it?'

'I should think that's obvious,' I replied. 'He disliked her.'

'Well, you don't like *hundreds* of people, but you don't go round bumping them off, do you?'

'No,' I said, 'but unlike F.O. I have more pressing things to do with my time.'

'Like dozing on your tombstone?'

'Exactly.'

It was quite apparent that Bouncer was getting more than usually above himself – probably the influence of O'Shaughnessy. The pair needed sitting on very firmly and I would have to devise some means. It could not go on.

35

The Vicar's Version

Fortunately my selection of the Herrick poem was well received, and the literary aspect now settled we could turn to the music itself. This was less onerous (for me at any rate) for the task of composition was put jointly in the hands of Tapsell and Jenkins. The partnership did of course produce a certain amount of friction but I kept my distance trusting that out of tumult something good would come. As in fact it did. Perhaps the stimulus of clashing egos had stirred their creative energies and lent lustre to the approaching days of winter. Whatever the reason, the end result was really a very tolerable piece of music which expressed Herrick's words most sensitively. Everyone was pleased and I found myself contemplating the ceremony of the Memorial Prize with unexpected cheer.

It was, however, a cheer somewhat compromised by Nicholas Ingaza. Two weeks before the event, he telephoned. I was surprised by this because once the binocular business had been settled and March (if not Samson) satisfied there was no further mileage in that direction, Nicholas had rather slipped from my mind. But not apparently me from his.

'Hello! Hello!' he oiled. 'Thought I'd just see how things were going. Had any good *sightings* recently?'

I laughed wanly and said that the little problem was all but cleared up and I was indebted to him for his help.

'I should think so, dear boy. I perjured myself black and blue with those charmers!' He chuckled. 'Produced a very spruce pair of Zeiss glasses for them *and* the wretched case, and said I'd just got back from Minsmere where thanks to my good friend the vicar I'd had a most productive time. Babbled on about curlews and Lesser Spotted this and Greater Spotted that ... bored them silly! You owe me one, old cock!'

'Well, Nicholas, if there's anything I can ever do...' I replied nervously.

'Not at the moment there isn't – but you never know, one day perhaps.' I felt relieved and prayed the day would never come.

'But as a matter of fact,' he continued, 'I

was thinking I might take a little pre-Christmas jaunt up to your neck of the woods, sample the fleshpots of Guildford and,' he added ominously, 'take a nose round Molehill and see what exactly you *have* been up to. There's something in your life, Francis, that doesn't quite add up!' And again I caught the familiar strains of that thin nasal giggle.

'You really are absurd, Nicholas!' I exclaimed. 'I told you at the time, it was all a stupid misunderstanding – you know how obtuse the police can be. A storm in a teacup, all blown over. I lead a very dull life here which wouldn't interest you in the slightest! Besides,' I added quickly, 'there are no fleshpots in Guildford, it's one of the stuffiest towns in the Home Counties, not your sort of thing at all.'

'Oh, I don't know about that,' he said, 'it's all a question of knowing where to look. I've one or two contacts in that area – Cranleigh actually – it's simply a matter of local knowledge.' I cursed Nicholas and his contacts, they seemed to be all over the damn place! And then he said something which really had me worried.

'Anyway, talking of fleshpots, while I'm in your area, thought I might beetle over and look up old Horace Clinker – give him a bit of a Christmas bonus!'

'No!' I yelped. 'He's had quite enough bonuses already. I'd leave him be if I were you.' The last thing I wanted was Clinker being disturbed – at least, not by anyone remotely to do with me. And certainly not by Nicholas. I was still basking in the news that I was to be left unmolested in Molehill. If Ingaza came blundering along needling the bishop and raking up the past, it was short odds that he would blame me and engineer my removal to the Cairngorms.

'All right, all right! Keep your hair on, dear boy. It was just a festive thought. I'll leave you in peace – *pro tem* at any rate. Who knows what the New Year may bring!' he added gaily. 'Toodleloo for now...' And still chuckling he rang off.

I breathed a sigh of relief and comforted myself with the thought that his interest in me and Molehill was a passing whim, and that come the New Year he would doubtless be embroiled in far more diverting matters. Meanwhile there was the Fotherington Memorial to deal with.

The days passed and the time for which we had all been preparing was nearly upon us. I have to admit to being in a state of considerable tension. The event had not only been absorbing my imagination but also haunting me in a strangely unsettling way. Obviously for the practical reasons already outlined – i.e. as a means to deflecting suspicion – it needed to be a success. But somehow it went deeper than that. I desperately wanted it to go not just smoothly but with style, grace, even splendour. It had to be something which people would enjoy and applaud and to which in future years they would always look forward. At the time I did not really understand these feelings but just knew that the event had an importance beyond the merely practical. Now, with reflection and hindsight, I realize what drove me. But then, though puzzled at my own intensity, I just wanted the thing to work; wanted it so much!

The Day came. Jenkins had rehearsed his choir until the music was pouring out of its collective cassock, and twirling his baton expertly, he strutted on to the platform like a junior Beecham. Enthroned in his eyrie Tapsell too was in his element – shooting his cuffs, flexing his fingers, and bowing expansively to anyone careless enough to cast their eyes heavenwards. Parents and parishioners sat solidly in well-filled and well-heeled ranks. The Vestry Circle's flowers looked untypically lovely, the silver glinted, the candles cast a mellow glow. And then at last the coughing and shuffling subsided and murmur gave way to an expectant quiet.

Slowly and rather stiffly I mounted the pulpit steps, placed my hands on its solid ledge, and fixing the congregation with solemn eye took a deep breath and declared: 'Now we will sing the Elizabeth Fotherington Memorial Anthem. All please stand!'

36

The Cat's Memoir

The afternoon of the Choral Prize-Giving had been a tranquil one for me. Not only was the vicar absent from the house but Bouncer too. As a special treat he had been allowed to accompany F.O. both to the event and to the supper afterwards. Despite the painful drama of the Fotherington soirée he likes that sort of thing – being petted and made much of – and is in his element when the centre of attention especially if there's food about. Thus for a few soothing hours the house was my own and I savoured the comfort of the fireside undisturbed.

Their return put paid to that. Both were voluble so I gathered things had been a success. Indeed F.O. was in an unusually expansive mood, singing what seemed to be a cross between a Te Deum and 'Ain't Mis-behavin''. As a means of relief you would have thought that such lyrical effusions would suffice. Not at all. Changing from his warblings into some sort of fractured chant, he swept me up in his arms and proceeded to foxtrot across the room. I am not used to being so manhandled and endeavoured to make my position clear. However, my protests were ignored and for some minutes (and much to Bouncer's obvious relish), we continued to zigzag and feather our way around the carpet.

Finally such indignity came to an end, and after calling me a 'silly old puss' he returned me to the rug and cavorted off to bed. Just occasionally it occurs to me that the dog was right – our master really is off his chump.

In the ensuing silence I turned to Bouncer and said as coolly as I could, 'I deduce from that performance that the occasion went well.'

'Oh yes!' he said. 'It was a very sparring evening – most sparring. I like a good tune, sort of churns you up, you know. You missed a treat!'

'I doubt it,' I rejoined irritably. 'I've been churned up more than enough for one evening! In fact I am beginning to feel distinctly queasy.'

Needless to say that didn't receive any sympathy. Instead he launched into a particularly puerile ditty:

'Quick, quick! The cat's being sick.'
'Where? Where?'
'Under the chair.'
'Hasten, hasten! Fetch a basin.'
'Too late, too late–
He's gone and done it in the grate!'

On the last word he keeled over with a howl of mirth and engaged in his usual leg-waving antics. I waited patiently for it all to subside – and was about to remonstrate when he bounded up off the floor and in solemn tones said, 'You know, Maurice, I think we may be safe after all. I think he's pulled it off! F.O. has put back–' and he took a deep breath – 'the STATUS QUO.'

'Great Fish!' I exclaimed. 'Where did you

get that from?'

He sniffed and in a chilly voice replied, 'You are not the only one around here who can speak foreign. I too have Classical leanings!' And taking his rubber ring in his mouth, he walked stiffly out of the room. As I sat pondering this extraordinary utterance I heard the rattle of the pet-flap and concluded that it was to be one of his nights for the crypt.

And then of course it became clear: it was the crypt that was inducing those 'Classical leanings', that gave him access to a dead language amidst the sleeping bones; the crypt with all its old tombs and plaques covered in their Latin inscriptions! So that was what he did down in the depths when he wasn't chasing spiders or at his baying practice: sat and stared at the crumbling stones and their grave and fading epitaphs; absorbing the words, sniffing the past. Cobwebs, it seemed, were not the only things that he picked up there.

I wondered if he was right about F.O. restoring the status quo. One would like to think so. It was getting a little wearying having all these Ponds and Marches traipsing in and out of the house; and if the recent display was anything to go by it wasn't doing the vicar's nerves much good either. A small respite might be a help to us all.

Two days later it was Christmas Eve and O'Shaughnessy came visiting. He was carrying a fresh and meaty bone in his mouth which he dropped at Bouncer's feet, then he grinned all over his foolish face. It was clearly intended as a Christmas offering and while as you know I do not approve of bones, it was nevertheless a kindly gesture and I commended the setter for his thoughtfulness.

'Hold on,' he said, 'got something for you too – won't be five ticks.' And he bounded off in the direction of his house. We waited in some curiosity. He returned soon with another object in his mouth. It was yellow and it smelt exquisite.

'Got this out of her shopping bag,' he chortled. 'Thought it might be right up your street, Maurice.'

It *was* up my street. It was a beautiful, shimmering, shining piece of haddock! A piece of haddock the like of which I had not encountered for many a month, and I seized it with a long mew of delight. We thanked him profusely for his Celtic kindness and said we would take him something very special on Boxing Day.

'That's all right,' he said. 'Just tell me when our *next* mission is to be. That was a grand thing so it was, that little outing to the woods!' I explained that we hadn't got anything immediately planned but living with the vicar one never quite knew when fresh reinforcements mightn't be called for. He nodded eagerly. 'Rightho!' he barked. 'I'll be off now.' And with a wild leap he cleared the fence and set off down the road in a lolloping career.

Bouncer gazed after him in rapt admiration, head tilted on one side and tail slowly twitching. I sighed, closed my eyes, and thought: 'Now I have *three* of them to contend with!' As I dozed I could hear myself purring. I cannot imagine why.

37

The Dog's Diary

It's funny the way things turn out. When Bowler rushed off like that I thought it was the end of the world. But I am very glad I came here, it's all been very nice. My first master was all right but he would keep *on* so! F.O. is much easier. Daft as a brush of course

– but then Maurice is peculiar too, and sometimes doesn't half talk a load of old bones! Still, I am managing to cope with the pair of them and generally holding my own.

I tried that long word on Maurice the other day, the one Bowler was always using. It had the most funny effect: it stopped him talking! It was quite hard getting it all out in one go but I managed it in the end. He was prosing on and on like he does and as I didn't have my rubber ring with me I was getting a bit bored, so I said it: *Mydeargoodlady!* He stopped in mid-sentence and gawped at me with his ears twitching and mouth wide open. I thought he looked pretty daft and was going to tell him so but I suddenly felt a bit sleepy and must have dozed off. Oddly enough he's never mentioned it since. Mind you, I still don't know what it *means* – but if that's the effect it has I might try it again sometime.

Christmas was good. We had a very musical time – with F.O. killing the keys in clouds of smoke and gin while Maurice ponced about on the piano-top like a regular old beauty queen! (I think deep down he's getting to like the vicar's playing though of course he'll never admit it.) On Boxing Day F.O. gave him a pale blue floppy bow and tied it round his neck. Knowing Maurice you would think he'd go berserk. Not a bit of it! He wore it the whole day long (even when it got all screwed up and scraggy), and I kept catching him making sly faces in the mirror and preening his reflection in the kitchen window.

F.O. also kindly gave me a new rubber ring. It's all clean and bouncy and I like playing with it. But nothing beats my old one, and although F.O. *thinks* he has got rid of it, I was able to drag it out of the dustbin and have put it in ANOTHER very secret place! This means I can take a crafty chew whenever the spirits move me (which they do pretty often) without the Man or the Cat ever knowing. No fleas on Bouncer, you know!

38

The Vicar's Version

It is always reassuring to see good coming out of ill. The ceremony of the Memorial Prize seemed to give pleasure to everyone. The boy chosen for the award was visibly moved by the experience (though later sufficiently recovered to hog the entire batch of Mrs Savage's fairy cakes and to mow down Mavis Briggs with his racing-bike prize). Tapsell and the choirmaster were much applauded for their fine piece which had been most ably rendered by the choristers, and were overheard eagerly discussing plans for further collaboration. Such sinking of base antipathies in the interests of high art is really most cheering. Uplifting too were the large banknotes stuffed into the Donation Box by satisfied parents and those still shocked by Elizabeth's demise. The Spire Fund derived enormous benefit.

I was a trifle sorry not to see Violet Pond in the audience – presumably preparations for the house sale being too distracting to allow attendance at her mother's commemoration. However, it was gratifying to glimpse in one of the back pews the bulky figure of Inspector March nodding gravely at some of the finer points of my address. Samson I could not see.

Thus the business of Christmas got off to a good start and the period passed very agreeably. It was hectic of course what with extra services, house calls to make and bazaars to open; but at least these were routine duties and gave welcome relief from some of the things I had been facing in the last six months.

These latter miraculously seemed to be resolving themselves: the police matter mercifully closed (or at any rate, with the help of Robert Willy, put into indefinite abeyance); the awful daughter decamped in dudgeon; and not a squeak out of Clinker. Was that even keel which had so stabilized my early weeks in Molehill beginning to reassert itself? Could life really be creeping back to being pleasant again?

I lack the knack of popularity but was nevertheless struck by the way people were beginning to hold me if not exactly in esteem, at least in kindly regard. Some of the parishioners had even been nice enough to produce seasonal gifts of brandy butter, cigarettes, tolerable mince pies and other friendly tokens. Such attention was surely less to do with my personal magnetism (of which, despite Elizabeth's peculiar yen, I fear I have little) as with approval of my recent donations. But I think some of it also stemmed from my having no special theological or social axe to grind. Thus I posed no threat to St Botolph's congregation, indeed was possibly seen as a handy aid in the preservation of its conservative comfort. Despite the unfortunate vicissitudes of recent months the future could perhaps be congenial after all...

With these thoughts in mind and to celebrate the imminent arrival of the New Year I poured myself a small malt and put on the gramophone record Primrose had given me for Christmas.

To the obsessive yet soothing notes of Bach's *Goldberg Variations* I stood at the window chewing a slice of Miss Dalrymple's heavily impacted plum cake and watched Bouncer as he bounded about with his new toy. The garden, which was never much even in summer, looked gaunt, and the gate and palings decidedly dilapidated. Come the spring I really ought to do something to spruce things up... Perhaps Primrose could suggest some new shrubs. But in the meantime I might certainly paint the gate and get some fresh fencing. Yes, that was obviously what was needed: a good smart fence. Probably Savage knew about such things, I would ask his advice.

I was half expecting a call from Primrose, so when the telephone rang I answered it eagerly meaning to raise the question of the shrubs. It was not my sister, it was Nicholas.

After the usual seasonal greetings he said, 'By the way, Francis, you remember you kindly said I might ask a favour of you?' The question was clearly rhetorical and he continued breezily undeterred by my silence. 'Well, there's a small thing that's cropped up where you might be able to help. It's to do with a couple of paintings I happen to have – rather good ones, not *un*valuable actually.' He paused.

'It's no use trying to sell them to me,' I said hastily. 'Don't have that kind of money.' (Not since my 'munificence' I certainly didn't!)

'Oh no,' he laughed, 'you've got the wrong end of the stick. I don't want to flog them to you, I'd just like you to keep them.'

'What do you mean, *keep* them?'

'Just for the time being while I find somewhere suitable – sort of safe storage really. You won't need to hang them on the wall,' he added quickly.

Miss Dalrymple's cake which a few moments ago had seemed so satisfying had somehow lost its savour and I returned it to the plate. 'Why can't you store them yourself?' I asked, beginning to feel my mouth go dry.

'Oh, I would,' he said airily, 'it's just that I

301

haven't the room at the moment, far too much clutter! They're for one of my more special clients but he's in America and won't be back for a few months. Until then they need rather careful handling by someone reliable, a safe pair of hands you might say; which is why I thought of you, Francis...' I stared ruefully at my hands, wondering wearily why people kept saying they were so damned safe.

He continued talking cheerfully, suggesting dates and times when the goods might be delivered. And I continued to stare out at the garden watching Bouncer and contemplating the sagging, broken-down fence. The dog was joined by Maurice who, clearly in one of his lighter moods, started to caper skittishly around the sun-dial. They made a pretty picture and I envied them their freedom, their peace...

I sighed. 'Yes, Nicholas, that's all right. Bring them next Friday at eleven. I'll be here.'

The publishers hope that this book has given you enjoyable reading. Large Print Books are especially designed to be as easy to see and hold as possible. If you wish a complete list of our books please ask at your local library or write directly to:

Magna Large Print Books
Magna House, Long Preston,
Skipton, North Yorkshire.
BD23 4ND